Ransom Town

The editor of the Fortrow Gazette, *a man who was usually a little less harassed than he looked, read the message for the third time.*

'O.F. S.E. needs money to help it fight for justice for the underprivileged so Fortrow's going to provide it. We'll set a small fire to prove we're in business, and then the price is a million pounds. Pay up fast or the fires get bigger, and after each one the bill doubles.

'Use the front page of the Fortrow Gazette to say the money's ready. We'll be in touch over the hand-over—make certain all the details of this are exactly carried out. Don't leave things too long or it'll get real expensive and a lot of people will find life becomes too hot for comfort.' It was signed Organization for Social Equality.

Genuine or the work of a mentally deranged person?

Other titles in the Walker British Mystery Series

PETER
ALDING

Ransom
Town

WALKER AND COMPANY · NEW YORK

First published in the United States of America
in 1979 by the Walker Publishing Company, Inc.

This paperback edition first published in 1983.

ISBN: 0-8027-3046-9

Library of Congress Catalog Card Number: 79-63635

Printed in the United States of America

10 9 8 7 6 5 4 3 2 1

I

They finally broke through into the bank's strong-room at four-fifteen on Monday morning, 9 June, barely inside their deadline. By then Barnes, an exaggerative pessimist, had been telling them for well over two hours that the job was bust and for well over two hours they'd taken it in turns to tell him to belt up.

Allsopp, the originator of the job, was the first to wriggle his way inside: the other four followed closely because although each man claimed to trust his companions, each wanted to make quite certain none of the others made a quick dive unseen.

The strong-room was fifteen feet long, twelve wide, and nine high. The walls and ceiling were painted a light green, supposedly to offset any tendency to claustrophobia: across one corner, stretching from wall to ceiling, was a cobweb which had trapped so much dust that the strands looked string-thick. At the far end were shelves which were stacked with suitcases, boxes, small crates, and even holdalls. Customers' valuables. The contents of those could easily double the amount of the cash, which was their primary objective.

The notes were in neatly stacked green canvas sacks and it was immediately obvious that there were more of these than their information had led them to expect so that their take was likely to be greater than the projected five hundred thousand. The sacks all had eyelets through which were threaded steel locking bars, pad-locked and sealed.

Allsopp took hold of one of the sacks – it had a pink label, showing it was filled with old notes to be returned for pulping – and began to lift it. Immediately a siren, ululating violently in that enclosed space, began to wail.

The plans hadn't listed a weight alarm, set in the floor. Goddamn it, they thought in that first moment of shock, the plans hadn't listed any such alarm. It wasn't fair.

Then they ran. The other alarms which they'd by-passed were connected direct to divisional police H.Q. so almost certainly this one was as well. They had about two minutes in which to get free.

There was a scrimmage at the hole they'd torn through the reinforced concrete lining of the vault and the brick wall of the cellar beyond because Barnes and Queen couldn't decide who was going to have the privilege of leaving first. Queen used his feet and won the point and Race somehow managed to get past Barnes. Allsopp was the last out, not on the analogy of the captain leaving his sinking ship, but because the others had beaten him to it. He still had hold of the green canvas sack with the pink label.

They left the ironmonger's by the back door and piled into the stolen Granada, parked in the courtyard. Barnes, who could be clumsy at other times, was an expert driver and he had them out of the courtyard in ten seconds. They were just clear and apparently pro-ceeding about their lawful occasions when the first police car, blue light flashing balefully, raced past them in the opposite direction.

2

Rain lashed the window with a splattering sound and Detective Inspector Fusil stared out to see distorted images. A better than usual November, the long-range weather forecast had suggested.

There was a knock on the door and Detective Constable Yarrow entered. 'Some more bumf from H.Q.' He placed several papers on the desk. 'By the way, sir, I've had word through that the factory job in Blind Lane may have been Old Tommy Manderton returning to business.'

Yarrow usually managed to irritate Fusil. He was not only bumptious and cocky, two characteristics which always annoyed the D.I., but on top of that he took great care frequently to remind everyone that he was a nephew of the detective chief superintendent at county H.Q.

Yarrow said briskly: 'I'll check up on that report, sir, and let you know the result.'

Fusil grunted an acknowledgement.

'Terrible weather. What price a quick flip out to Barbados and the sun?'

What price? wondered Fusil sourly as he watched Yarrow leave. With all the upheavals which had occurred when the Fortrow borough police force had been swallowed up by the county force, it should have been possible to 'lose' Yarrow – yet he was still around, still knowing all the answers, even to unasked questions.

Fusil sighed. Intolerance was said to be an infallible sign of old age. He opened one of the drawers of the desk and brought out his heavily charred pipe and filled the bowl with tobacco. He lit the pipe and when it was burning freely he leaned back in the chair and thought about the amalgamation of the two forces. It was surprising how so much change had resulted in so few changes. He was still in command of eastern Fortrow C.I.D., although now it was called K division and the area had been extended to take in some of the surrounding countryside. Divisional H.Q. remained in the same outdated, overcrowded buildings, and finances were still too tight for any of the long-delayed alterations and modernizations to be carried out – now more necessary than ever because the establishment numbers had been raised. No new typewriters had been issued, nor had any portable tape recorders, the number of civilian clerical staff was even more inadequate in the face of an ever-growing mountain of paperwork. . . .

He picked up and leafed through the papers Yarrow had left on his desk. Notices, lists, memoranda, requests for information, statistics. . . . An army marched on its stomach, the police force pounded along on its bumf. He came to the last sheet of paper. Origin, Detective Chief Superintendent Menton's office: question, was there anything more to report on the bank robbery at Mattock Cross which had taken place in July?

That robbery, so very much less successful than the villains must have planned, had taken place before the amalgamation of the forces and so 'Babs' Browning of J division had been in charge of the investigations. Very little progress had been made. Fusil drew on his pipe. He and Browning had joined the force within six months of each other. He remembered that when they'd first met he'd judged Browning to be a person who thought rules were promulgated in heaven: nothing in Browning's subsequent career had caused him to amend that derogatory judgement.

When a D.I. took over a new divisional C.I.D. he did so with the advantage of an unwritten, but much honoured, law: the cases still on the books (i.e. unsolved) were omitted from subsequent statistics of crime figures so that in this way one man's record was not saddled with another man's failures. The only exception to this was when the incoming D.I. actively pursued such investigation when, of course, the case would have to be brought back into the statistics at the obvious risk of depressing the all-important clear-up rate.

Fusil held the pipe away from his mouth and watched the thin column of smoke rise, to be very quickly shredded by one of the many draughts which whistled through the room. He'd naturally read the file on the bank robbery within hours of taking over K division. One fact had stood out like a sore thumb – the villains had had inside information. He hated traitors.

Every time a bank robbery went unsolved, two more were undertaken, because crime, like any other business, followed success. And bank robberies were always potentially violent. So if the Mattock Cross job remained unsolved, sooner or later innocent people might suffer vicious injuries in a subsequent bank robbery as a direct consequence of the police's failure. . . . He'd taken on the case. He claimed to be a self-honest man, always ready to step back and examine himself and his motives. But inevitably there were some areas which he did not examine very closely because subconsciously he was reluctant to do so. So it was that in this instance he

9

carefully didn't ask himself whether in truth his decision to keep the case open was not, in part at least, motivated by the far less laudable desire to black Babs Browning's eye by succeeding where the other had failed. . . .

He picked up the internal phone and called Campson into the office. 'Sit down, Sid.' He didn't often use Christian names.

Detective Sergeant Campson sat. He made a quick adjustment to his tie and then folded his arms. A man in his early thirties, he was already beginning to bald so that his hair had receded to leave a widow's peak over his long, rather pointed face.

'Reference the bank job at Mattock Cross,' said Fusil. 'How's it stand?' Campson was just as efficient as Braddon had been and he possessed considerably more imagination and initiative, but Fusil would have far preferred to have had his old detective sergeant back. Campson was another Babs Browning – always checking on what was supposed to be done and what was not supposed to be done.

'In what particular respect, sir?' asked Campson, in his deep, musical voice. He was equally unhappy to be serving with Fusil because sharp unorthodoxy must mean trouble sooner or later.

'You worked with Mr Browning on it: how far did you get?'

Campson knew Fusil must have read the papers. 'Not very far, sir. The mob were real professionals and didn't leave behind a single lead which ripened.'

'There was one which should have done. They were fed inside information.'

'Naturally, we reckoned that. But when we checked the background of the staff there was only one man who looked promising and he turned out to be in the clear.'

'You can't have dug deeply enough.'

'Mr Browning had us digging down to the bottom and we still came up with the same answers. There's no shadow of proof of anyone having fed the mob the details of the alarm system.'

'Damnit, a blind man couldn't miss the signs. The mob knew exactly which wires to cut to immobilize the main alarms and the plans of the original system were kept in the strong-room: the mob didn't know about the weight alarm which was installed two years later and the plans of this weren't in the strong-room.'

'There must have been several copies of the original plans.'

'Of course. So where are they? In the architects' offices? In the installing firms' offices?'

'We checked out that angle, sir.' Campson's voice hinted at a sense of resentment: J division hadn't been manned by a pack of fools, K division didn't now contain all the brains. 'We decided there couldn't have been a leak either from the architects or the installing firm. So we reckoned the mob were just plain clever at their work.'

'The easy way out!'

Campson flushed. 'We thoroughly examined all the possibilities. . . .'

'But obviously not thoroughly enough. I want the bank staff turned over again. Sooner or later, the traitor will panic.'

'You're going to reopen the case, sir? But we checked and re-checked . . .'

'You and me will get on like a house on fire when you learn that the only time I push a case to one side is when all the villains concerned are under lock and key.'

'Yes, sir,' said Campson tightly.

'O.K. Get things moving just as soon as you like.'

Campson stood up. 'There's just one thing, sir. We've enough work on hand to keep two of each of us busy. If I have to detail men to backtrack on this case some of the current work is going to have to be put on one side. . . .'

'No, Sergeant, no work is going to be put on one side. We're just all going to work that little bit harder.'

Campson left.

.   .   .   .   .

The letter arrived in a greyish envelope addressed merely to the *Fortrow Gazette* so it was opened in the general office to find out to which department it should be sent. The twenty-year-old secretary, who'd just had her hair re-styled and wasn't quite certain whether she now liked it, slit open the envelope and brought out a folded sheet of paper. She read the typewritten message. 'Hey!' she said. 'Get a load of this.'

'Got another of *them*, have we?' said the blonde. 'The town's overflowing with dirty old men.'

'No, it's not like that at all. Come over and read it.'

The blonde left her desk and crossed the cluttered floor, having to step round a pile of old magazines. She picked up the letter and read it. 'Twice round the bend,' she said, with all the certainty of sophisticated in-experience.

'But what department does it go to, Dulcie?'

'Send it to that old cow in Production. It'll scare the pants off her.'

She sent it up to Editorial.

.   .   .   .   .

The editor of the *Fortrow Gazette*, a man who was usually a little less harassed than he looked, read the message for the third time.

'O.F.S.E. needs money to help it fight for justice for the underprivileged so Fortrow's going to provide it. We'll set a small fire to prove we're in business, and then the price is a million pounds. Pay up fast or the fires get bigger, and after each one the bill doubles.

'Use the front page of the *Fortrow Gazette* to say the money's ready. We'll be in touch over the hand-over — make certain all the details of this are exactly carried out. Don't leave things too long or it'll get real expensive and a lot of people will find life becomes too hot for comfort.' It was signed Organization for Social Equality.

Genuine or the work of a mentally deranged person? The paper received a number of letters from crazy people in the course of every year and so he had had some experience of them: the style of this letter made him think it was not in such category. He reached over for the outside phone and dialled divisional H.Q. When the connexion was made he asked to speak to the detective inspector, to be told that Mr Fusil was out.

'Blast!' he said, having wanted Fusil's snap judgement on the letter. 'Look, ask him to give me a ring as soon as he gets in, will you? The paper's received a letter which he needs to know about.'

He said good-bye and replaced the receiver. If the police accepted this letter as potentially genuine, they'd check it for prints so it shouldn't be handled any more than it already had been. But the *Gazette* must have a copy for its own records. He called his secretary and told her to get the letter copied, but to be careful to handle it only by its edges.

3

Fusil studied the envelope and letter, to which was attached a slip saying 'Checked out for dabs'. There would have been a number of prints and all these would have to be compared against those of the people known to have handled the paper: the odds against finding an unidentified print of consequence was too small to be considered at this stage.

The postmark was Newcastle and the date of franking that of the day before. The quality of the envelope was ordinary enough for it to have been bought in any one of thousands of retail outlets. The typing was regular and the type clear.

A fire and then a million pounds or a second, larger fire and after that the ransom was two million. Inconsequentially, he remembered the story of the Arab who was offered a reward and because he was 'very modest' he asked only for one grain of wheat for the first square on a chess board, two for the second, four for the third. . . . How many billions of grains were needed for the last square?

Was this the work of a nutter? It was astonishing how many sick people wrote letters threatening, pleading, exposing, or prophesying. But their letters were usually prolix and egotistical in nature and this one was to the point and impersonal. No, he decided, this probably was not from a nutter. He re-read it, very slowly, trying to gain the flavour of the words. Was it from some terrorist organization, as its signature suggested? Apparently. And yet . . . For the moment, he couldn't fully formulate what caused his doubt.

He checked the number, dialled the *Fortrow Gazette*'s offices, and asked for the editor. 'Bob here. Thanks for getting in touch with me about that letter. We're checking it through now, of course . . . No, no real conclusions at this stage, but I'll go so far as to say I don't think it's from a nutter. . . . Yes, I'll be getting on to the anti-terrorist squad. . . . Now that's one of the things I wanted to talk over. I know you'll be dead eager to print, but hang back, will you? Look at it this way, Fred. Print the letter and a lot of people are going to get the wind right up, with reason. After all, if someone wants to set fire to a building, he's tens of thousands of targets to choose from and right now the police haven't a hope in hell of stopping it. So if I'm wrong and this turns out to be from a nutter after all, then all those people will have been scared half to death for nothing. On the other hand, if it's genuine we've a lot of things to get organized before we can properly cope with the public's reactions. . . . Yeah, I know I'm asking you to cut your own throat, or suffocate, or whatever. But you play along now and next time a town councillor is found in bed with a fourteen-year-old schoolgirl I'll give you a head-start on the story. . . . Thanks a lot.'

He replaced the receiver. He telephoned county H.Q. and spoke to Detective Chief Superintendent Menton, head of C.I.D.

'No, sir, I reckoned to report to you before getting on to London but they'll tell me if this O.F.S.E. outfit is known to them. Can't say I've ever heard of it before. . . . Yes, I'll get straight back on to you. . . . Dabs are working on the letter now.'

Menton, a man who couldn't help being over-precise, asked several questions which Fusil reckoned totally unnecessary before ringing off. Fusil then telephoned New Scotland Yard and asked to be put through to the Anti-Terrorist section. He spoke to an inspector and briefly described events. 'Have you come across the Organization for Social Equality before?'

'It doesn't ring any bells right away, but hang on and I'll check.'

He waited, tapping on the desk, as always impatient.

'Hullo... No, we haven't met it before. But nowadays that doesn't mean overmuch: sometimes it seems as if every other day there's a new outfit sprung up and trying to get in on the act, shouting for this, that, *and* the other. You've nothing else to go on: no background, no idea of what they're really after or what other outfit they might have contacts with?'

'No.'

'Leave it with me, then, and I'll ask around. In the meantime, I presume you'll be calling us in?'

'As far as I know, yes.'

'Someone will be down, then, but God knows who — we're so short-staffed we've forgotten what time off means.'

'Snap.'

The inspector laughed. 'Oh, well, as I always comfort myself, we may die from perforated ulcers, but it won't be from boredom.'

.   .   .   .   .   .

Detective Constable Kerr, standing in front of the large, leather-topped desk, ran his fingers through his brown, curly hair as if to try to shake some order into it. He smiled disarmingly. 'I know just how you feel, sir.'

The bank manager, a thin, sniffing man, sniffed. 'I doubt that. Perhaps you are unaware that this must be the fourth or fifth visit from the police I have suffered?'

'I'm afraid these things usually do drag on for a long time.'

'Surely, though, not for months?' Detective constables were becoming even younger and brasher, the manager decided sourly.

He hadn't been asked to sit, but Kerr sat. 'It goes like this. We reckon the mob must have had inside information which means a member of the staff was either bribed or blackmailed into giving it. If it was blackmail, that won't show up in the man's accounts, but if it was bribery, then it probably will. If the regular house-keeping money isn't drawn for a few weeks, or there's a large cheque paid in . . .'

'Constable, would it not be possible to credit me with an understanding of the more simple financial facts of life?'

Kerr grinned, making him look younger than his twenty-four years and underlining the fact that there wasn't much in life which he took too seriously. 'Then that saves me trying to explain. . . . Do any of the staff's accounts look at all interesting?'

' "Interesting" is hardly the word I would use.' The manager rested his elbows on the desk and joined his thumbs and finger-tips together: he stared at Kerr over the top of the triangle formed by his fingers. 'As you may know . . .' He sniffed. '. . . All bank staff are obliged under the terms of their contracts to maintain their banking accounts with their own bank. I therefore am fully conversant with all the accounts of my staff and I can state quite categorically that not a single one of them shows any noticeable variation in income or expenditure.'

'Not even that of Brian Morgan?'

'I believe I said, not a single account.'

'That's one lead unfortunately closed right up, then.'

'It is strange to hear honesty regretted, Constable.'

Kerr grinned again. 'It's just that in our job obvious dishonesty makes life a lot easier.'

'No member of my staff is dishonest. No member would ever have passed on any information concerning the alarm system.'

'I'm sure you're right, but we have to keep on plugging away. What's this bloke Morgan like?'

'Why do you keep referring specifically to him?'

'Because he did raise his life style after the robbery: colour TV, a new car, a holiday abroad with his wife . . .'

'All of which is – as I would have thought you knew – readily explainable. His father-in-law gave him a present of three thousand pounds. At the beginning of this very protracted investigation, the selfsame point was raised with me and I was able to confirm that a cheque for that amount drawn on his wife's stepfather's account was paid into his account.'

'I wish my father-in-law could afford to slip me three grand. . . . And you can't help me turn up something in anyone else's finances?'

'I cannot.'

'Thanks a lot, then. With any luck I won't have to disturb you again.'

Kerr walked along the High Street, then stopped in front of one of the show windows of a large furniture store. On display was a sectional, curved sofa, in light green. Two nights ago, he and Helen, after leaving the cinema, had walked past this store and she had suddenly come to a stop and stared at the settee and after a while she had said, in a wistful voice: 'If only we could afford that. It's just what I've been wanting ever since we were married.' He would have given anything to be able to go inside and buy that settee on H.P., but the deposit alone would have wrecked their budget for months. He ought to have gone up to the Midlands to work in one of the car factories: no discipline, no excessive and often unpaid overtime, no fear of having to face an armed and desperate villain so that a hospital bed or a grave was just a hairbreadth away, but instead a wage which would buy any settee his wife wanted. . . . He was not a very deep thinker, being a person who largely lived for the present, but he did sometimes wonder about the paradox by which modern society most devalued the work of those on whom it most relied to maintain its standards.

He turned away from the show window and as he did so a Ferrari, blood red, its exhausts growling money, came to a momentary stop abreast of him. The driver was about his own age. The line of traffic moved once more and the Ferrari continued on its golden way into the late afternoon which was already turning into dusk. Some people enjoyed a very different world. Was the driver on his way to pick up a luscious blonde who was both promise and delivery? Would they eat in a restaurant where the prices were so high that the average man's wallet would faint at the sight of them? He suddenly laughed aloud. What the hell! Life played more jokers than aces. In half an hour's time, that epicene driver might be a gory mess after trying to do eighty round a thirty corner.

He continued past several expensive shops to the

traffic lights, where he turned right. Here there had been no need for major reconstruction after World War 2 bombing and the shops were small and old-fashioned and some of them were obviously having to struggle really hard to meet the competition of the supermarkets and chain stores.

At the police station he went up to the detective sergeant's room which lay between the D.I.'s and the general room.

'Sarge, I've been to the bank. There's nothing fresh on offer. The manager swears none of his staff could have passed on information and all their accounts are whiter than white.'

Campson spoke with bored superiority. 'I could have told you that before you started.'

'Why didn't you, then, and save me the journey?'

'It was the old man's picnic.'

For once, Kerr maintained a tactful silence. One didn't have to be very perspicacious to understand that the detective inspector and the detective sergeant would never see eye to eye over how to run the divisional C.I.D. 'Do you want a report on the interview?'

'That's a bloody silly question! In triplicate, with all the underlining in red.'

'I'll be off, then, and get it started.' He looked at the clock on the wall: three-quarters of an hour before he could safely finish work.

'See Morgan when he gets back home,' said Campson. 'Question him about his life style – how he managed to go to Crete for his holidays when most of us can't get any further than a grotty hotel in Mallorca.'

'Sarge, that's all been sorted out long ago. His wife's step-father gave them three thousand smackeroos The bank statements have been checked and Coutts did

20

draw a cheque for three grand on his own account . . .'

'Mr Fusil wants it all checked again.'

'But what's the point? What can I ask that's fresh?'

'You'll think of something – you're never short of words.'

' "Their's not to reason why . . ."? All right, I'll see him tomorrow morning and . . .'

'You'll see him this evening,' cut in Campson, with pleasurable authority.

. . . . .

The Dutch barn was to the right of the old-fashioned farm buildings in an area cleared from the rough woodland which stretched north to the Heathcote road. When full, it held three thousand bales of hay.

The wind came from the south-west, harassing the remaining leaves which stubbornly clung to the branches of deciduous trees. A number of yews grew near the Dutch barn and their needle-laden branches threshed against each other to make a noise like that of distant, heavy surf.

On the south face of the hay in the barn there appeared a quick flame. A gust of wind bent this flame right over and seemed to extinguish it, but seconds later it reappeared, grown astonishingly. Within fifteen minutes, flames were rising higher than the ridge of the main span.

4

D.C. Welland had earlier made it clear that in the course of duty he needed the C.I.D. car from six o'clock onwards, but he wasn't a man to hold a grudge for long, so Kerr used the car to drive to the north-western suburb of Dritlington.

He parked close to number fourteen, Clevis Road. It was a road of semi-detacheds, each with a small front garden and a slightly larger back one. The kind of housing into which a detective superintendent might retire if he'd been careful with his money all his life.

The front garden of number fourteen, seen in the light of the nearest street light, was immaculately tidy with not a weed or a dead leaf in sight. It reminded Kerr that he really ought to do something about their place, as Helen kept suggesting: but gardening irritated him because it was literally never-ending – one couldn't ever sit back and say, 'Well, that's it.' He rang the bell and heard a short chime.

The door opened. He couldn't remember when he'd last seen a woman who so immediately reminded him of rumpled sheets. She was carefully built and her main attractions were obvious but not ostentatious. Her eyes were dark, velvety brown and her lips were very full and moist and they curled as if to ask 'When?' 'Mrs Morgan?' he asked, in what he hoped was a level voice.

'Yes?'

'My name's Detective Constable Kerr. I'd be most grateful for a quick word with your husband, if that's at all possible.'

'I suppose so,' she answered, with obvious reluctance. 'But he really does like to rest completely when he gets back from work.'

If he came home to a wife like this, he wouldn't be at all concerned with resting. He smiled as he stepped inside. 'I promise to make it as short as I can.'

'Brian's out at the back, playing with his woodwork, so you'd better come through. I'm afraid the kitchen's in a bit of a muddle.'

He followed her across the attractively furnished hall and through the kitchen. When he wasn't watching the voluptuous way her hips moved, he noticed that the kitchen had all the latest labour-saving machinery. A wife who'd have made Miss Troy *and* a generous Mr Coutts seemed to be overdoing one man's good luck.

The back door led out on to a small tiled area and the far side of this was bounded by a wooden shed, ten feet by six, from which light streamed through the single window. She opened the door, but at that moment a power saw created a shrill whine which made any speech impossible until the sawing had finished. 'Brian. There's a detective to see you.'

'Who d'you say was here?'

She ignored the question, turned, and walked back into the house. A man looked out of the shed. 'What's the matter?' Sawdust had sprayed the sweater he was wearing.

Kerr introduced himself and explained the purpose of his visit.

Morgan turned and pulled a plug out of its socket,

switched off the overhead light, came out and shut the door. 'I can't think what you want to talk about now,' he said petulantly.

'Just trying to tie up a few odds and ends.'

'I thought it was all over and done with. I suppose we'd better go into the sitting-room. . . . No, it'll have to be the dining-room because Betty will be watching the telly.'

Betty. What a totally inappropriate name! She should have been christened Penelope or Consuella.

The dining-room, not very large, was over-furnished. There was a mahogany leaf table with ball and claw feet, elegant but too heavy for the space, and six ladder-back chairs whose homespun style failed to suit the table. There was a sideboard with elegant brass handles, on the top of which was a large cut-glass bowl containing fruit, and a pair of four branch candelabra with fluted stems. On the wall opposite the fireplace was a heavy gilt-framed portrait of an elderly man with mutton-chop whiskers and the face of a petty tyrant.

'I suppose you'd like a beer?' asked Morgan. Then, realizing he'd hardly framed the question politely, he hastily added: 'Or some sherry, if you'd prefer that?'

'I think I'd like a sherry, please. When it gets this chilly, I go off the beer.'

'If you're cold, I'll put the fire on.'

Morgan bent down and switched on a fan heater. He was a well-built man, with a broad pair of shoulders and a slim waist. He had tight curly hair, heavy eyebrows, a pleasantly shaped nose, a regular mouth, and even, white teeth. His smile was engaging. Yet Kerr saw in his face an underlying suggestion of weakness which prevented his being handsome.

Morgan crossed to the sideboard and brought from

this two glasses and a half-filled bottle of sherry. He filled the glasses and handed one over. 'Move a chair out and sit down. I'm sorry we're stuck in here and aren't in the other room, but Betty wouldn't miss her programme for anything and you know what the ladies are – you have to keep 'em happy.'

It would take a real man to keep her happy. Kerr raised his glass 'First today and twice as welcome for that.' He sat down. 'As I said, I just wanted to find out if you could tell me anything fresh about the bank robbery?' He looked enquiringly at Morgan.

'But I thought that was finished with weeks ago?'

'I wish it were – then right now I'd have my feet under my own table and not be bothering you. . . . No, I'm afraid we're still trying to find out who the villains were and how they learned the details of the alarm system.'

'I'm sure . . .' He stopped. 'I just don't believe any of the staff would ever have given away the details of the alarms.'

'That means you can't think of anyone who might have done such a thing?'

'It means I wouldn't even try,' replied Morgan, with an attempt at firmness.

'Not if you *knew* someone on the staff was a traitor?'

'I don't know and nobody knows that for certain, so it's a hypothetical question.'

'But an interesting one, perhaps?'

Morgan drank.

'You've a nice place here, Mr Morgan . . .'

'Look you don't have to beat all around the bush. You're forgetting, I've been through all this before.' His voice rose. 'I'm just an ordinary bank clerk so I don't earn enough to buy a new colour TV, a new car, and go on holiday to a nice hotel in Crete, all within a few months. Where did the money come from? From telling someone where the alarms were? No, it bloody didn't come from there, because I never told anyone anything. Betty's step-father gave us three thousand pounds because we're young and he reckoned we'd get more fun out of it than he could. There's nothing illegal there, so why keep persecuting me?'

'Steady on, no one's persecuting you. We always have to check up on everyone in a case like this and find out who's spending. But the moment you explain where the money came from, that's it – there's an end to everything.'

'No, there isn't. I've explained everything before and it's been checked, but now you're here, still poking and prying.'

'Call it force of habit. What I really came for is to find out whether you've heard of anything fresh which might help us.'

'To put things more crudely, will I be an informer?'

'If by that you mean someone who'll help us arrest the traitor, yes.'

Morgan emptied his glass, hesitated, then stood up and crossed to the sideboard to pour himself another drink. 'It's the way you people are so ready to believe I *could* be a crook which gets me. Why?'

'Well, for one thing, crooks don't always come with stubbled chins and bad breath.'

'What's that supposed to mean?'

'That it doesn't matter what anyone's position is, he can't be above checking out. If there were a leak of information from our department, I'd expect to be under suspicion, along with every other member of C.I.D., until the traitor was found, even though I'm

26

every bit as proud of my own honesty as you are of yours.'

Morgan drank. He wiped his mouth with a handkerchief. 'I'm sorry,' he mumbled. 'I didn't mean to be rude.'

'There's no call to be sorry,' said Kerr, slightly contemptuous of the sudden unnecessary and ingratiating apology.

'But I shouldn't get so hot and bothered about being questioned. As you said, everyone's got to be under suspicion until you find out what happened. I'm sure you're wrong, though. No one on the staff would have told the crooks about the alarms.'

'Well, maybe we'll know one way or the other some day. In the meantime, let's have a recap – do you know anyone on the staff whose life style has changed very much for the better?'

'There's no one like that. Because there's no traitor.'

'You're very loyal,' said Kerr. He stood up. 'Thanks for the drink.'

'That's all right. And I'm sorry if I seemed to get a bit excited, but . . . Well, you know how I feel. Look, have the other half before you go?'

'Thanks, but I'll be on my way. Supper should be waiting and I could eat a couple of horses.' He put his glass down on the table and realized he'd made a mistake when Morgan hastily came forward and picked it up. 'Betty likes to keep things clean.'

Pity! thought Kerr.

•   •   •   •   •

On its south side the suburb of Ribstow was bordered by the Old Docks. A Salvation Army captain had once declared that in the streets of South Ribstow the Lord

27

and the devil fought face to face. Certainly, the chief occupation of those who lived near the docks seemed to be either relieving visiting seamen of all their possessions or else stealing or receiving cargo. Vice was a way of life, violence and theft were endemic, and virtue was a foreign word.

However, within this jungle there were some clearings and the further north one went the larger the clearings became. Near the borders of South Flecton there were a number of houses, often run by retired prostitutes who possessed the necessary toughness of character, where men (seldom women) could for a very reasonable amount rent a bed-sitter for the day, week, or month, and lead an uneventful life.

Mrs Prosser had grown stout, but it was a jolly fatness, a celebration of the honest life she had finally reached. With this honest life had come a liking for respectability and now it was only when she had been drinking that she forgot to guard her behaviour and acknowledge her partiality for young men. Unfortunately, she drank rather a lot.

She looked at her watch. It was already eleven-thirty and she swore, a habit of which she could never break herself. She went into the hall, newly polished because cleanliness was next to Godliness, and stared up the stairs. 'Bert,' she shouted, her voice hoarse from chain-smoking.

An elderly man, bald except for a few straggly grey hairs, looked over the banisters upstairs. 'I ain't seen him around at all, Ma.'

'Give him a shout: the lazy bastard can't have got out of bed yet,' she said with good humour. She had a soft spot for Albert Mickey because he reminded her of a pimp for whom she had once worked.

She walked over to the mirror by the side of the elaborate coat-stand and studied her reflection. She was well satisfied with what she saw.

There was a wild shout from above. ''Ere. Ma, come 'ere.'

'What the hell's the matter?'

'Oh, Gawd!'

It was obviously serious. She hurried up the stairs, beginning to pant before she reached the top. The old man was in the doorway of Mickey's room, looking inside. 'What is it?' she demanded roughly. When he didn't answer, but just continued standing there, she pushed him aside with a sweep of her massive hips.

The bed was an old, iron-framed one with heavy uprights topped with brass balls, candy-twist framework with scrolls, and springing of the most primitive type, all now rusty and chipped. A looped length of cord had been tied to part of the largest scroll and Mickey's head was inside the loop, his distorted face turned towards the door. His body sprawled out at an angle, so that his feet extended clear of the right-hand upright.

5

Fusil said, 'All right, we'll look into it,' curtly enough
to make it clear that he thought the supermarket
manager's complaint was of little substance. He left the
office and impatiently pushed his way through the
crowd of shoppers to the outside doors. His car was
parked on double solid lines and a traffic warden was
preparing to write a ticket. 'Bad luck,' he said, 'but
this is one you don't make.'

'Oh, it's your car, Inspector! Well, you know, we're
supposed to book everyone who parks here, even if
they're from C.I.D. . . .'

'If you're down on numbers for this week, try
Ponders Road.'

'It's not that. But it is narrow just here and a parked
car does cause the traffic to slow up. . . .'

Fusil climbed into his car. He knew he'd behaved in
a boorish way, but didn't give a damn. The small-
minded exercise of authority always annoyed him;
that was why he worked badly with some of his superiors.

He drove along to the traffic lights, turned left, and
threaded his way through the back streets to the main
Barstone Road. Once clear of the town, he reached
over and picked up the radio microphone with his left
hand and pressed down the transmitting switch. 'Hullo,
Sierra Sierra X-ray. Has anything fresh broken? Bravo
Tango one, over.'

'Hullo, Bravo Tango one. There is a reported male suicide by hanging from Ribstow.'

'Are any details in?'

'Not yet.'

'Who's gone from C.I.D.?'

'I think it was D.C. Yarrow.'

'Anything else?'

'Nothing of any consequence, sir.'

'I'm on my way to county H.Q. I hope to be back by fifteen hundred hours. Over and out.'

A man had hanged himself. What torments had driven him to that? Fusil could see himself committing suicide if suffering from an incurable disease and to do so would be to release his family from the heavy burden of his illness, but in no other instance because he believed every man should have the courage to fight through to the end. Yet he was not blind to the fact that strength of character must to some extent be dependent on security. The man with a family and home was so much better armed than the man who was alone and homeless: the selfish man was better armed than the compassionate one. Had this man lacked any security so that he had surrendered when if he had had it, he would have fought? If so, who with security had the right to call him a coward? . . .

. . . . . .

Kerr parked by a call-box. He climbed out of the car and although the wind was keen and he had not brought an overcoat, he stood for a moment enjoying the scene. In front of him was a playing field, with a few houses on either side, and beyond this the land dipped away: by the time it rose to come in sight once more, it was all fields. Hedgerows held oaks and ashes, newly ploughed fields were geometrically patterned, winter wheat was a sharp green. One day, he and Helen would buy a place in the country, fulfilling a long-held ambition of hers. He finally turned away and entered the call-box.

Because he was in a foreign division, he rang their H.Q. and asked the detective sergeant if it would be all right if he had a word with Henry Coutts, who lived in Mayfield. After a bad-tempered beginning – all detective sergeants seemed to develop a jealous possessiveness with regard to their territory – he was finally given permission.

Coutts lived in an old farmhouse, with peg-tile roof, red/blue bricks set on a ragstone base, exposed beams in the inside walls and ceilings, and a large inglenook fireplace in the sitting-room. 'Sorry to bother you like this,' Kerr began breezily, 'but we're having to check up yet again on the bank robbery back in July.' He grinned. 'You probably know what authority can be like: tell 'em the same thing twice and they demand to hear it a third time.'

Coutts, an elderly, thickset man with heavily featured face, dressed in polo-neck sweater in a Fair Isle pattern and grey flannels, said: 'That doesn't really explain why you've come to see me again.'

'Well, it's like this . . .'

There were several sharp knocks on the floor above which sounded loudly below because the floorboards were set directly on the beams. 'That's my wife,' said Coutts. 'She's . . . rather ill so I'd better go up and see what she wants. Excuse me a moment.'

The tone of voice and Coutts's quick expression of anguish told Kerr that Coutts accepted she was dying. Kerr seldom concerned himself with other people's

32

troubles, but as Coutts left the room he did wonder if he could have shown such self-possession had Helen been dying. He shivered. There were times when a policeman was forced to learn that life could be very red of claw.

He heard footsteps cross the floor overhead, the quick creak of a bed, and a murmur of voices, the woman's petulant in tone. After a while, the footsteps recrossed the floor. Coutts returned downstairs.

'I'm sorry about that. Do sit down. Now, what's the trouble?' Coutts crossed to the rather small window and stared out at the lawn.

'After the bank robbery the police had to make the usual kind of enquiries and this meant checking up on all the staff because it did seem possible that someone had told the villains the layout of the alarm system. One way of checking up . . .'

'Let me cut you short. You are looking for someone whose standard of living has risen sharply. In the past few months Brian Morgan has bought a new television set, a new car, and he and Betty went to Crete for a holiday in the summer. So where did the money come from?' His voice was flat and expressionless. He turned round. 'I explained some time ago to another detective. . . .'

There were several more knocks from above.

Coutts looked up at the ceiling, an expression of tired resignation on his face. 'I'm very sorry,' he said, speaking in the same level voice, 'but I'll have to go upstairs again.' He left.

Kerr heard the wife talking, the words indistinguishable, but their querulous import obvious. Feeling cold, and this was not wholly a physical experience, he stood up and went over to the fireplace in which several logs

33

were burning on firedogs set over a bed of ash. He studied the various knick-knacks set out on the mantelpiece, which included a triptych of family photos. A much younger Henry Coutts, his face alive with fun, stood with a woman – he was in a dark suit, she was in a smart frock and hat and she held a posy of flowers in her hands: their wedding day? A boy and girl were sitting on the far side of a table, in a garden, laid for a birthday tea: he looked about fourteen, she about twelve and her sexuality was obvious despite the clumsy clothes she wore – had Betty been a Lolita? A dog, a mixture of terriers, looked up at the camera and grinned, plainly ready for any devilment that was offered.

Coutts returned. 'I'm afraid my wife is not at all well today.' He made the statement so unemotionally that it was obvious any expression of sympathy would have been very unwelcome. 'I see you've been looking at those photos. When we take them, we never seem to realize how badly they may hurt years later.' Just for a second, his self-possession slipped and his mental agony showed. Then he regained control of his emotions. 'You're here to ask the same old questions? Do you expect anything but the same old answers? I gave my stepdaughter and her husband three thousand pounds in the summer and told them to go out and spend it all on luxuries. They're young and can enjoy luxuries: my wife and I can no longer do so. It was all done legally and with due regard to all our iniquitous tax laws. Surely you know all these facts?'

'Yes, but we do have to check.'

'To check the checking? If the police have already made certain that I did give Betty and Brian three thousand pounds, why return here to ask whether this was so?'

'I'm afraid that's the way police work often goes.'

Coutts shrugged his shoulders in a gesture of tired indifference. Kerr remembered earlier asking Campson what was the point in covering the same old ground. Campson hadn't been able to give a reasonable answer either.

Kerr was saying good-bye when the knocking started yet again. He was glad to get out into the cold, windy air, away from the woman who tapped away her remaining life.

.   .   .   .   .

Detective Chief Superintendent Menton, standing, said in the tones of a peevish toast-master calling the roll of honour, 'This is Detective Inspector Lancome from A.T.' The two men vaguely resembled each other to look at because both had thin and authoritative faces, rather secretive eyes, and heavily lined foreheads: but any closer similarity was prevented by the mouths, Menton's suggesting a cold, distant character, Lancome's a warm, cheerful one.

The other three greeted Lancome each in his own manner: Detective Superintendent Weal with a measure of condescension because he was always very conscious of rank, Detective Chief Inspector Adams with a brief, 'Hullo, haven't seen you in fifteen or sixteen years,' and Fusil with no more than a couple of words.

'Let's sit down,' said Menton, as if bestowing a favour.

The four chairs had been carefully grouped around the large desk in a semicircle and on each was a single foolscap sheet of paper. Menton, behind the desk, said in his colourless voice which could become so boring after a while: 'Fusil, you'd better give us the latest report.'

'Nothing much to add, sir, except that we've started making all routine enquiries. But, first off, I would like to discuss the letter.' He tapped the sheet of paper which had been on the chair before he sat. 'I don't think this is from a nutter – the style's wrong and the details, as far as they go, too practical.'

'I imagine we all agree with that.'

'So it would be reasonable to assume it's from a terrorist gang who call themselves the O.F.S.E. They're trying to hold Fortrow to ransom to obtain funds. The scale of the operation seems larger than usual, by which I mean it's a whole town which is threatened and not any individual target, but I imagine that that's quite conceivable?'

Lancome said easily: 'It's difficult these days to conceive what isn't conceivable.'

Weal nodded his head vigorously. 'A bloody H bomb It's going to happen one day.'

Menton looked annoyed by so extreme a flight of the imagination.

Fusil said: 'So the letter's from a terrorist organization or from villains being paid to do a job by terrorists. . . . Or from villains masquerading as terrorists in order to scramble the trail.'

'There's not much contact between the two parties,' said Lancome. 'They each hold the other in pretty deep contempt.'

'Then that leaves terrorists or villains. I think we're dealing with villains.'

'Why?' asked Menton.

'When I checked with A.T., they said they'd never heard of the organization.'

Lancome answered the point. 'I don't think we should try to read too much into that. These days everyone with a grudge sets up as a terrorist, threatening to burn and blast. Brand-new organizations are two a penny. We can't keep track of 'em all.'

'But surely you'd at least have heard a whisper before an outfit reached the stage of going into a production this big?'

'Not necessarily. I think I'd better make a point here. Terrorists are a different species from villains, not just a different breed. We all know there's something in the average villain which drives him on to seek the admiration of his fellows and so, for instance, he spends like money's going out of fashion just to show he's Mr Big. The average terrorist does just the reverse. He wants to be Mr Nobody, so he moles away, hiding as hard as he can. I'm perfectly prepared to learn that here is a terrorist organization, the O.F.S.E., about which we haven't previously heard a single whisper.'

'That seems clear enough,' observed Adams.

Fusil said: 'Then take the letter. There's to be a little fire to show they're not fooling and then bigger and bigger ones if we remain unconvinced, screwing down the pressure. That's the psychology of a professional.'

'Why can't a terrorist be professional about a crime?' asked Weal.

'No reason at all,' answered Lancome.

'If he's professional in attitude,' objected Fusil, 'he must have been around to learn. Then surely A.T. would have heard of him?'

Menton said: 'A man doesn't have to have had twenty years' practical experience to work out the most effective way of forcing people to meet his demands.'

'Maybe not, sir. But wouldn't the amateur terrorist which by definition is who we're dealing with – be

37

more likely to start off with a thumping big fire to hammer his point home and then threaten another as big or bigger?'

'The sledgehammer rather than the subtleties of ever-increasing threats,' said Weal, who was inclined to make a point after it had been made.

'If I were to look for subtlety,' said Lancome, 'I think I'd be more inclined to look for it in the terrorist than the villain. Generalizing – which we must – the villain comes from a background where education is scorned while the terrorist so often comes from a background of good, even very good, education. Which makes one wonder whether education really is as valuable as it's cracked up to be.'

No one bothered to comment on that.

Fusil said, now sounding a little weary: 'There's a sick humour in the letter.' He tapped the sheet of paper. 'The ransom doubles after each fire. That's the kind of threat which would really appeal to a villain. And the letter ends by saying people will find life getting too hot for comfort. A villain would laugh his head off at that play on words.'

'Why shouldn't a terrorist have a twisted sense of humour?' asked Adams.

They looked at Lancome.

'I suppose,' he said, making it clear that this was a point over which he wasn't going to be very definite, 'that since a terrorist usually manages to convince himself that what he is doing is justified whereas the rest of the world knows it is horribly unjustified, he must be mentally twisted. So why shouldn't he have a twisted sense of humour? But in my experience, terrorists are notable for a complete lack of any sense of humour, twisted or otherwise.'

'I wouldn't describe this as a very valid point,' said Menton.

'All right, sir,' said Fusil stubbornly, 'I can't give a single reason which stands up to argument. But my instinct still says that this letter comes from villains, not terrorists.'

'We need more than instinct to go on.'

Weal, who fancied himself as a committee man, said: 'In practical terms, how important is the point right now?'

Lancome answered him. 'That's very hard to answer. If we know we're dealing with terrorists, we concentrate on identifying their cause and likely sphere of association because this should give an indication of their background and whether they'll have been in touch with other, known organizations: if we're certain we're dealing with villains, it's the old established routine of checking up on names that C.R.O. picks out and also offering an attractive reward for a good grass. But I wouldn't have said that these two lines are necessarily exclusive.'

'Of course not,' agreed Weal.

'They are if someone decides to make them so,' said Menton.

Fusil understood that he was being rebuked. Probably he shouldn't have been quite so definite: Menton needed leading, not pushing. But in this case he was certain that as far as the police were concerned there wasn't time for very much subtlety.

.   .   .   .   .   .

Fusil arrived back at divisional H.Q. at a quarter to four, three-quarters of an hour later than he had hoped. 'Too much waffle and not enough do,' he muttered as he parked in the reserved space, but he knew that his annoyance was directed at himself and not at his three senior officers and the D.I. from A.T. It wasn't often that he couldn't quote chapter and verse for his conclusions.

He went into the building through the back way, along a dimly lit corridor which smelled of damp and humans, and up the back stairs to his room. There was a note on the desk asking him to call Mr Harvey.

''Afternoon, Bob. We've had a letter arrive by the afternoon post. It's very short so I'll read it over. "You've had the first instalment. The price right now is a bargain – just one million. Hang around and the pace gets hotter." It's signed the Organization for Social Equality again.'

'Quite the humorist!' Here was confirmation of what he'd told them, he thought – that sly, twisted, sneering contempt for humanity and authority. 'Where's the postmark?'

'Fortrow Central, so the letter was posted in the middle of town. The paper and the envelope look the same and memory tells me the typing's also the same.'

'Thanks a lot. I'll get a bloke over right away for the letter. By the way, what did the fire brigade say about last night's fires?'

There was a short, dry chuckle. 'Aye, I have been on to 'em. They had six fires last night, full reports of which haven't all come in. Anyway, they were a bit cagey with me and wouldn't say if they suspect arson. They'd only go so far as to admit none of the six was classified as a major outbreak.'

'Right now we're looking for a minor fire, aren't we? The one that persuades us that their threat's genuine so we hand over the million?'

'Bob, I can't hold back any longer. I'm going to have to print.'

Fusil began, 'Can't you . . .' then stopped. It was unrealistic to expect the paper to withhold the news any longer. 'O.K., but keep it really low key, will you? None of this scaring everyone into next week.'

'We don't need to make the idea scaring, do we? It starts off that way.'

After the call was over, Fusil rang the fire service. The fire investigating officer was out, but he would be asked to ring back as soon as he returned.

Fusil filled his pipe with tobacco and lit it. A high-rise block, violent fires, stairs, service and lift shafts drawing the fire up with explosive speed, electricity gone, panic . . .

6

'You know, of course,' said the pathologist, as he stared at D.C. Bressett through the upper half of his bifocals, 'that death is caused by vagal inhibition, cerebral anoxia, or asphyxia, if a ligature is tightened around the neck?'

D.C. Bressett didn't know or care. He hoped he wasn't going to be sick.

The pathologist bent closer to the naked body which was stretched out on the tiltable autopsy table. 'Hum!' he remarked.

Bressett struggled to think of anything but the man who lay on that table with screwed-up eyes, twisted nose, curled and sneering lips, and protruding tongue on which teeth had clamped down in one final spasm of agony.

'Interesting!' said the pathologist. 'Give me a six.'

His assistant, a suitably morose-looking individual, handed him another knife with a long, curved handle.

They hadn't mentioned attending post mortems in the recruiting advertisement, Bressett thought resentfully. 'D'you want to do a man's job and feel ten feet tall?' Right now, he felt ten inches and rapidly shrinking.

'It's interesting how many people believe your feet have to swing clear of the ground before you can hang. Pure nonsense. Any number of the people who hang themselves – often accidentally – do it with part of their legs touching the ground. Last year I had a case of a young man who hanged himself sitting. Know how it happened?'

Bressett didn't answer.

'He dressed up in women's clothes, went out into a wood, spread out a few girlie magazines, fixed a rope to a tree and put a loop round his neck. Masochists seem to gain considerable pleasure from putting their heads into loops: flirting with the ultimate pain, I've heard it called. It's the only kind of flirting that kind of person does – what?'

Bressett shivered.

'The rope pressed deeper into the neck as he moved around and shut off the arteries. He was unconscious before he knew anything was happening – anaemia of the brain. Then asphyxia set in and it was all over.'

Bressett knew they'd rib him mercilessly back in the hostel because they knew he was squeamish. Had his first P.M. gone with a real swing? Did he know there was spaghetti for supper?

Some twenty-five minutes later, the pathologist crossed to the double sink, stripped off his long gloves and green overalls, changed from green wellingtons into shoes, ran hot water into one basin and scrubbed his hands with antiseptic soap. He used a fresh towel to dry his hands with pernickety care. He spoke to Bressett after he'd dropped the towel into a bin. 'We've an interesting case here: very interesting.' His words occasionally bore the trace of a burr. 'I've taken samples of his blood and urine, of course. I expect to hear that the blood alcohol level is fairly high.'

He began to pace a small section of the floor which stretched between the table on which the body was now being stitched up by his assistant and the basins. 'D'you

43

know anything about strangulation?' he asked suddenly and sharply, much as if he had been giving a lecture and wanted to find out if one of his students had dozed off.

'Not really, sir.'

'Well, it's an interesting subject.' 'Interesting' obviously denoted approval. 'In hanging, a ligature usually has a knot to form the loop that goes over the head and this knot sticks out proud and imprints itself on the neck.

'The knot will either have been on one side of the neck or at the back. If it was at the back the whole face will be pale, if it was on one side the face is often red on that one side only because of the complete compression of arteries and veins there. Consequently, if one finds the face is pale on the one side of the knot, one starts asking oneself questions. . . . Where was the knot in this case?'

Bressett was forced to look closely at the corpse. 'On the left-hand side.'

'Yet the left-hand side of the face is pale, isn't it?'

Would he ever forget that tortured face?

'So we have to start asking ourselves some interesting questions. Of course, in my report I shall state only that there is a reasonable possibility that this was not suicide. Proof, one way or the other, will have to come from other sources.' The pathologist came to a sudden stop in his pacing. 'What about the rope?'

'The rope?' repeated Bressett stupidly, conscious that his stomach was now in open revolt and a cold sweat was prickling his forehead.

The pathologist looked at him and it was possible to imagine there was a glint of amusement in his eyes. 'The rope with which he was hanged could be of considerable importance. Was a careful note made of the exact way in which it ran over the bed?'

'I . . . I expect so, sir.'

He checked the time. 'Well, that's that, then. I've another P.M. to do in a couple of hours' time – a very interesting case indeed. Come back and watch it.'

Bressett swallowed quickly, then shook his head.

.   .   .   .   .

Fusil was in the front room when the call came through and the duty sergeant handed him the telephone. 'Mr Jepson, sir, fire brigade.'

Jepson had a high-pitched, reedy voice which fitted his thin, ferrety face and his prominent Adam's apple. 'I gather, Inspector, you want to know about the reported fires last night and whether any of them could have been arson? Well, there's one possibility and that's a strong one.

'A Dutch barn, almost full of baled hay on Beanpole Farm in Wrexley Green. The alarm was given at twenty-two forty-seven hours and the local pump appliance was there by twenty-two fifty-nine hours. They were unable to bring the fire under control but as there were no other buildings near-by there was no need to call out any more appliances and the fire eventually burned itself out.

'Now, as to the cause of the fire. The main question is, was it spontaneous combustion? That normally occurs only between eight and eighty days from cutting the grass and this grass was cut between early May and middle June. Another thing, with spontaneous combustion the heat builds up in the interior, giving a noticeable and characteristic odour, and the fire begins

45

in the interior and works its way outside. I've spoken to the farmer and he's quite definite that since they started taking hay a fortnight ago there's been no odour and when he first saw the fire the outside was in flames and the top inner bales were still not alight. This fire was either accident or arson.'

'Right. I'll get a bloke out to question the farmer and his men.'

'I've had a word with him and . . .'

'I'm sure you have, Mr Jepson, but we'll have to make the further enquiries for ourselves. Thanks a lot for your help.'

He said good-bye and rang off. If words were valuable, some men would be millionaires. He called Yarrow to his room.

'Get out to Beanpole Farm in Wrexley Green and check on the fire they had last night in their Dutch barn. You're looking for proof of arson because the hay couldn't have gone up on its own.'

'Right, sir,' said Yarrow, in a tone of voice which suggested that now that he was on the job all would soon be clear.

If only Yarrow didn't like himself so much, thought Fusil with fresh irritation.

. . . . .

Yarrow drove in the C.I.D. Hillman to Wrexley Green, a village situated around cross-roads which consisted of a pub, a general store, and half a dozen cottages. An elderly woman on a bicycle – she reminded him of his dusty Aunt Ethel who had spent much of her life sucking peppermints – directed him over the cross-roads a mile further on, past a couple of bungalows and a lot of scrub woodland.

46

He parked in front of the house and since the front door was obviously seldom used, he walked round to the back door. A dog chained to a kennel barked several times, after which it retreated inside the kennel to escape the raw wind. Yarrow knocked on the door, then stared at the woods which came up to the end of the sodden garden: bare trees, a tangle of bracken, bramble, and weed grasses, and overhead a cawing crow. One had to be half dead to want to live in the country.

Old Farmer Giles, as Yarrow immediately christened the man who opened the door, was large and fat and cheerful: put him in a smock and give him a straw to chew and he'd fit snugly into any rural Christmas card. His wife, no less large and no less cheerful, offered Yarrow a mug of coffee.

'It certainly were a blaze and a half,' said Ochett. Just for the moment his cheerfulness deserted him. 'A hundred tons and most of it real good: no fill-belly there. Had to work hard for that hay, seeing as it was always showering. We were in the fields turning as soon as the dew was off, we'd bring the baler in when the sun was well up, and then like as not there'd be a bloody shower just strong enough to muck everything up.'

Yarrow was quite uninterested in the trials and tribulations of hay making. 'Was the hay insured?'

'Oh, aye. But hay's short this year and what I insured it for won't be buying me in a hundred ton of the same quality, that's for sure.'

'Any ideas why it caught fire?'

'Some bloody fool put a match to it, that's why.'

'Why d'you say that?'

'When I make hay, it don't go up in spontaneous combustion. And none of my blokes would smoke round

47

by the barn. So some silly bugger set fire to it and if I get my hands on him . . .'

'You leave that to the police, Fred,' said his wife.

'That does a power of good, don't it? If they catch him, like as not he'll end up with probation. Too soft, that's what this country is now. I'll tell you how to cure this bastard. Send him here next spring and make him work on next year's hay. He won't set fire to no more barns after that.'

Yarrow could appreciate the bitter anger which came from seeing so much hard work destroyed, but appreciation did not lead to sympathy: he seldom felt sympathy for the misfortunes of others. 'Have you any idea who might have a grudge against you? Maybe a farm worker you've sacked . . .'

'I ain't sacked a man in years because I've always chosen workers. None of them kind what want paying for just sitting and looking. As I always tell 'em, I'm the bloke who takes all the risks, but don't get a paid holiday every year. . . .'

Farmers were all the same. Pleading poverty, but always with a brand-new Rover in the garage.

•   •   •   •   •

A cynic had once said that any informer who claimed his motive was public duty was about to ask for a better rate for the job. Fusil disagreed because he had known one or two who'd informed for reasons which came close to a sense of social duty, but he'd felt contempt for even them because he hated traitors, no matter what it was they were betraying.

He leaned against the side of the call-box and closed his eyes: he was achingly tired, eager to fall asleep on his feet.

''Ullo,' said a sharp voice.

He identified himself. 'I want a lead on the mob who's trying to screw this town by threatening to burn down a building full of people. There's some heavy bunce for the right answers.'

'I ain't heard anything. But I'll keep listenin', mister.'

As he rang off, he visualized Joe: a guileless face, making him look like someone's favourite uncle. He'd always accepted payment, but would never ask for it. Why? Fusil didn't know.

He left the call-box and returned to his car. With any luck, he'd only be a couple of hours late home.

7

As Fusil approached his office on Thursday morning, Miss Wagner came striding along the corridor. 'Mr Fusil,' she called out. Most people guessed her age at around fifty, but she was younger than this. She was, unfortunately, not an attractive woman: she had a large mole on her chin from which grew three long and very noticeable hairs, her upper front teeth protruded, and her nose was beaky. But if not atttactive, she was at least highly efficient at all things she undertook and in addition she was a professional survivor, having even survived the amalgamation of the two forces and the order that all civilian employees of the borough force were to be paid their redundancy money and removed from the strength.

Fusil went into his office and sat. Miss Wagner, her face expressing a certain annoyance, came to a halt in front of the desk. 'Mr Fusil, I called to you just now,' she said, rather breathlessly.

'I'm sorry, I was thinking hard of other things.' When he had first been appointed D.I. in the borough force, he had found that she had virtually been running the administrative side of the C.I.D. for years. Exercising a degree – for him, a great degree – of tact, he had firmly made her return to purely secretarial duties. She might have been expected to resent such a reverse, even to the point of resigning, but in the event she had quietly accepted the situation without any apparent resentment. Fusil had soon found her so trustworthy that he had begun to give her work more pertinent to the position of a personal assistant than a mere secretary and before long she was once more handling administrative matters. It had been a curious and interesting example of the quirky circles that human relations wove.

'Mr Fusil, there's a message on your desk. Mr Menton urgently wants a word with you. He's just rung again and he seemed a little upset that he couldn't speak to you.'

This was Miss Wagner's oblique way of telling him he had arrived late at the office. 'I overslept and Josephine left me to it instead of waking me.'

'I'm very glad to hear she did,' she said earnestly. 'But will Mr Menton be quite so understanding?' She sniffed.

'Did he suggest what was troubling him?'

'He'd only say the matter was urgent. I think it will be best if I get him for you right away.' She picked up the telephone, checked it was switched through to an outside line, and dialled county H.Q.

He hated being fussed over, but nothing would ever stop her fussing over him. He waited as she said over the phone, in her prim, official voice, that Mr Fusil wanted to speak to Detective Chief Superintendent Menton, please. 'Good morning, Mr Menton. I have Mr Fusil for you. Will you hold on for one brief moment, please.' She handed Fusil the receiver with a flourish, as if she had been personally responsible for this miracle of communication.

'Fusil, have you seen the *Daily Express* this morning?'

'No, sir.'

'They've splashed the story of the ransom letters. I've

already had I.T.N. on to me, demanding the full story. Why in the hell did you let the news leak out?'

They both knew that if a story were newsworthy there was virtually no chance whatsoever of keeping it under wraps. But Menton was a man to pull rank as a means of venting his annoyance.

'How's the ransom case look right now?'

Fusil detailed the steps which had been, or were about to be, taken. The two letters were with the forensic laboratory, who had yet to report; Dabs had said that there were no unidentified finger-prints on either. Word was being circulated to all the local grassers that there was heavy bunce for anyone giving solid information. National and county C.R.O. were checking their files for the names of all known arsonists.

'You sound as if you've now convinced yourself we're up against villains, not terrorists,' observed Menton sharply.

'Whether I have or not, sir, it doesn't mean I'm not liaising fully with A.T. They're completely in the picture.'

'I was speaking to Inspector Lancome a little earlier. He mentioned he'd half a dozen names that needed checking out. Have you taken any steps in that matter yet?'

'The photos are already up on the boards for identification and every patrol is being briefed before going out. . . . Incidentally, sir. Lancome told me that he still can't ferret out a single reference to the O.F.S.E.'

'Which doesn't mean a thing at this stage. You heard him say in my room that he's perfectly prepared to accept that there are terrorist organizations existing of which he hasn't heard even a whisper.'

'Yes, sir. Which is why I'm working to both alternatives. But I still see that as a bit of a pointer, considering the scale of this job.'

Menton asked a few more questions and then rang off. In theory, Fusil thought, Menton was right. The police didn't yet have anything approaching proof. But Menton had for a long time been more concerned with administration than with field work and it was field work which honed a man's instincts.

Campson entered the room and handed over a sheet of paper. 'The night crime, sir.'

Fusil skimmed through the typewritten list. Two housebreakings, one Peeping Tom, one (question mark) rape, three muggings, one serious wounding, one missing person, one floater from the harbour, one serious hit-and-run, three acts of vandalism. Because of the ransom threat, some of these cases would have to be turned over to the uniform branch. It was something he disliked doing intensely. He could delegate responsibility to his own men without worrying because he trusted them − or, to put it at its lowest level, he was certain he would find out in time if they began to make a hash of things − but he was sufficiently egotistical not to trust anyone who was not under his command. 'Keep back as much as we can handle and send the rest below.'

'They're pretty overworked as it is, sir.'

'They don't know what overwork means.'

Campson disapproved of such inter-departmental intolerance. There should, the Standing Orders book roundly declared, always be thoughtful liaison between the various branches of the force.

There was a brief knock and Kerr entered. ''Morning, sir,' he said breezily.

Campson's disapproval grew. In his book, quite apart

from the Standing Orders book, morning reports should be made through the detective sergeant who could then weed out all non-essentials at the same time as he made certain everyone was doing his job properly. But Fusil encouraged personal reports, making it seem he didn't trust his D.S. 'Is that all, sir?'

'Yeah.' Fusil said to Kerr: 'Well?'

Campson left, wishing he could complain without making himself look ridiculous about the lack of working respect the D.I. showed to his rank.

'I had a good sniff round in the bank job, sir,' said Kerr. 'One thing's for sure. Brian Morgan's wife is a very rich piece of crackling.'

Fusil briefly wondered if he'd ever been quite so carefree, even when he'd started in the force. 'D'you think we could forget the scenery and concentrate on the facts?'

'I suppose so, sir. I've checked and all the facts stand. Mrs Morgan's stepfather gave the couple three thousand quid and that's what upped their life style. The bank manager confirms that Mr Coutts gave them that much.'

Fusil picked up a plastic ruler and began to smack it up and down on the palm of his hand. The case belonged back in cold storage. It seemed ridiculous to pursue it any further when the city was being held to ransom. Yet to give a traitor best . . .

'There's just one more thing, sir. At one stage, I did get a sniff of a hint. Hanna, the assistant manager at the bank, was nervously eager to help. I've an idea there's something to be gained from pressuring him.'

Innocent people often were ill-at-ease when being questioned by the police, so that this was more a guess than a hint. But a good detective learned to guess correctly – and to call his guesses instinct. 'See Hanna and pressure him as far as you can safely. Do it tonight.'

'Tonight, sir?'

'After you've finished work.' Fusil grinned sardonically.

Kerr left and Fusil read through the mail. There were five requests for witness statements from outside forces and another three from within the county force. He swore. Each request represented a detective's time. . . .

There was a knock on the door and nothing happened until Fusil shouted out, then Bressett stepped inside. Fusil sometimes wondered whether Bressett would make the grade. He was good at his job, but he lacked drive and self-confidence: a good detective should be able to walk naked through a garden party at Buck House if he felt he needed to.

'We've received a report from the lab, sir, on the rope Mickey was hanged with. For part of its length the fibres are all directed upwards towards the loop which apparently means the rope was pulled over something solid when it had a weight on it: maybe Mickey was dragged up to the position he was found in. And as I mentioned in my report, the pathologist said that the face was white on the side of the knot when it should have been . . .'

'I remember. By the way, I like the way your report was made.' Fusil saw the quick look of pleasure on Bressett's face. 'So now it's become odds on we've a murder and not a suicide! All we bloody needed!'

'I'm sorry, sir.'

'There's no call to be. Unless you croaked him.'

.   .   .   .   .   .

Welland called for two more pints of bitter, something

which came naturally to him. The landlord drew the draught beer and passed the glasses across the counter. Welland carried them over to a table at which sat a small, wrinkled man, whose face was tanned by sun, wind and rain. 'Here you are, then. A bit of father's milk to make your toenails grow.' He sat, jolting the table because he didn't readily fit into the narrow chair. 'There's nothing like a pint of wallop to restore a bloke unless it's a couple.' He drank, then wiped his mouth with the back of his hand. 'You were telling me about this stranger you saw walking past Beanpole Farm and having a good look a day or two back. Can you describe him?'

'Oh, aye, that I can.' The small man drank with the eagerness of a large capacity. It astounded him that after sixty-two years, man and boy, he had at last met someone who was willing to buy him several beers without expecting any in return.

· · · · ·

Yarrow stepped out of the car and stared along the road with contempt. The docks were not far away, but even that didn't really explain why this street was so rundown: most of the small, mean terraced houses had peeling paintwork, rotting timbers, missing and cracked panes of glass, and broken tiles. Obscene graffiti were common, the road gutters were littered with rubbish, and there were two abandoned cars from which even the locals could find nothing more worth pinching.

He knocked on the door of number five. When there was no answer, he knocked again, impatiently, and finally the door was opened by a child of seven whose beautiful deep blue eyes held all the cynical knowledge of a woman of fifty-seven. 'Is Mr Casier in?' he asked, turning the word 'Mr' into a term of sarcasm.

She studied him. 'You ain't the rent man.'

'That's right. Look, if your father's in the house, I want a word with him.'

'He ain't my dad,' she said with sudden force, not bothering to explain what relationship existed within the home. ''Ang on.' She shut the door.

The door was opened by a shambling man whose once solid body had long since turned to fat. He hadn't shaved for a couple of days and stubble, tinged with grey, darkened his cheeks and chin. His clothes were rumpled and stained. He didn't know Yarrow, but immediately identified him as a detective. ''Ullo, mister. 'Azel said as you wanted a word?'

They went into the front room. There were empty beer cans on the mantelpiece and in the fireplace, cheap magazines lying about everywhere, rubbish on the torn and worn settee: an ashtray had tipped over and its contents were strewn about the floor. The room smelled of dirt and decay.

'Were you just passing by?' suggested Casier ludicrously.

'Give over,' replied Yarrow contemptuously.

Casier fiddled with his right sideburn, twisting the long hair into tight twirls.

'You've been busy recently, haven't you?'

Casier ducked his large, egg shaped head and smiled weakly. 'I'm always busy, mister. I've got this job down at the docks and . . .'

'Busy with the torch.'

Casier drew in his breath with a hiss and he blinked rapidly. His pudgy mouth, with thick curling lips, moved as if he were trying hard to speak.

'You've been knocked four times for torching.' When dealing with men like Casier, Yarrow never employed subtlety in his questioning: that would have been to credit them with some intelligence. 'You get your kicks from starting a blaze and then standing around and watching it. Better than a woman, isn't it?'

Casier ducked his head.

'So you've been giving yourself some more thrills recently.'

Casier said, with frantic emphasis: 'Mister, I ain't done nothing, I swear I ain't. I ain't touched a box of matches in months.'

'You've just torched a barn filled with hay. A real fire, with flames fifty feet up. Must have thrilled you weak.'

'I'm telling you, mister, I ain't touched no hay: I ain't torched anything.' Desperately trying to convince Yarrow he was telling the truth, he stepped much closer. Yarrow hastily retreated to avoid the fetid breath. 'I wouldn't never torch hay 'cause the animals eat it. I wouldn't never hurt an animal.'

As Yarrow studied the pudgy face, strained from the effort of trying to speak convincingly, he realized that, as absurd as it sounded, this was almost certainly the truth. Casier would set fire to a building in which were humans without a thought to their safety, but he wouldn't set fire to fodder because that would be to deprive animals of food. The human mind came in all sizes and shapes – mostly twisted.

8

Fusil stood in the centre of the room in number nine, Bretton Lane, and stared at the ancient iron bed with its candy twist framework with scrolls.

Bressett pointed with his right hand. 'The rope was over that cross-piece, sir, and the body was lying in this direction.'

What a way to die, thought Fusil: stretched out in a decaying bed-sitter.

He walked forward. At the point where Bressett had indicated, the lower curve of one of the scrolls had been rubbed by something and in one place the metal was showing bright underneath. He saw, close to this, the single fibre of material – almost certainly from the cord – which had been caught under a jagged edge of metal. 'Get a good shot of this,' he said to the third person in the room.

Detective Sergeant Walsh muttered something about the difficulties of obtaining a photograph when set against that background.

Fusil continued to stare at the bed as he said: 'You've been through his clobber – is there anything of interest in it?'

'No, sir,' replied Bressett. 'Some clothes which even a Steptoe wouldn't cart away, no papers of any sort, no letters or personal memoranda, no names or addresses. There was a wallet in his coat and that contained nothing but fifty-two pounds, thirty in tens and the rest in oncers.'

'Fifty-two?' said Fusil, surprised since a man reduced to Mickey's circumstances usually lived from hand to mouth. 'I wonder what petty skivering he'd been up to? . . . O.K., let's go down and see the lady of the house.' He turned and spoke to Walsh. 'Let me know how you get on with the dabs.'

'There won't be any worthwhile.'

'Some day, you're going to drown in your own misery.' Fusil led the way out of the room which, to anyone of imagination, was still acrid with the stink of death.

A man peered out from one of the other rooms as they went along towards the landing: when Fusil looked directly at him, he partially withdrew, his expression scared. Fusil wondered now much sadness, loneliness, tragedy, a house like this contained? How many of the blasted lives had once appeared so promising? Was fate the villain, or each man his own? He hated criminals with the sharpness of someone who believed in the Old Testament's unforgiving definitions of good and evil, but for wrecked lives like these he had a deep compassion in which good and evil could often not be separated.

Mrs Prosser was waiting in the front room. She had dressed with special care and her hair had recently been permed: her manner was grave and courteous. She had, however, been drinking. After greeting Fusil with the aplomb of a dowager, she said: 'Will you have a sherry, Inspector? It is nice and dry.'

'Thanks, I'd like one.'

She filled three glasses, not bothering to ask Bressett if he wanted one. She sat on the settee and sipped her sherry with ladylike sips to begin with, but then with far greater enthusiasm.

Fusil knew her record. Fifteen years ago she'd been a tart, tough enough to survive even in the toughest of districts. But she had fought through to late middle age and an apparent respectability, so Fusil was not going to deny her the fruits of this victory. He treated her as if her name had never appeared on a charge sheet. 'I'm very sorry we've had to come here and bother you,' he said. 'It's been a distressing time for you.'

She nodded in a composed manner, whereas had she commented aloud on events she would have done so in blasphemous and scatological terms.

'We'll get out from under your feet just as soon as we can, but we're going to have to check out one or two things. The trouble is, Mickey's death may not have been suicide.'

She was visibly shocked. 'What d'you mean? I saw him, swinging from the bed.'

'The medical evidence is that he may have been murdered and then tied against the bed to make it look as if he'd committed suicide.'

She finished her sherry in two quick swallows. Then she swore, which startled Bressett who'd naively accepted her as being the woman she portrayed.

'D'you know if Albert Mickey was his real name?' asked Fusil.

'When he came here he called himself Bert Mickey and there's never been no reason to think otherwise.'

'Any idea where he came from?'

'I didn't ask, he didn't tell. . . . Look, Mr Fusil, I'll give it to you dead straight. He just turned up one day and wanted a bed-sitter: he'd got the necessary, he didn't look wild, and so I said "yes". But I didn't

61

ask questions and didn't look around for no answers.'

'But you did get friendly with him?'

'Why not? He weren't Paul Newman, but he was company and he reminded me of someone what I used to know.'

'Did he take you out and about a lot?'

She laughed mirthlessly. 'You've got things round the wrong way. If I'd of waited for *him* to take *me*, I'd still be waiting.'

'Obviously, he didn't have much money?'

'It was a good week when he paid for his room. . . . I'll confess it to you, Mr Fusil, I'm getting soft. Even let him have the room on the slate more than once, just because he looked like this bloke I once knew.'

'Have you any idea what he'd got in his wallet when he died?'

'If it was an uncut quid, I'm surprised.'

'I'm going to surprise you a hell of a lot. He'd fifty-two quid.'

She stared at him for a moment, then she suddenly laughed loudly and her heavy jowls and pouter-pigeon neck wobbled. 'The old bastard!' she said with reluctant admiration.

'You'd no idea he'd that sort of spending clout?'

'I'd have given you fifty-two to one he hadn't. Just goes to show, don't it? Never too old to be taken for a sucker. If I'd known that, he'd have paid for a few of the meals when we went out, I can tell you.'

'Would you reckon he'd a lot of friends?'

'He'd chat with blokes, but I wouldn't say any of 'em were his friends.'

'What about lady friends?'

'Never heard of any.' Her tone of voice suggested

that if she had, she'd have done something about the situation.

Fusil finished his sherry. She heaved herself to her feet and refilled his glass and her own, but didn't bother about Bressett's.

'What kind of security have you got in this place?' asked Fusil.

'You're talking about the front door, aren't you? I tell all of 'em, eleven o'clock and the door's locked and unless I've given 'em a key they're out for the bloody night.'

'Then you don't usually bolt the front door as well as lock it?'

'That's right.'

'And where do you sleep?'

'In the room on the other side of the hall.'

'So you'd hear anyone coming in late – anyone you'd lent a key to?'

She hesitated. 'Mostly. But sometimes I sleep pretty solid. . . .' She stopped. She was tough in mind and body, but the point of the D.I.'s questions had been obvious and now she was scared because she visualized the murderer or murderers forcing the front-door lock – easy enough for any professional – and going upstairs during which time she slept so soundly she heard nothing.

Fusil drained his glass and stood up. 'We'd better push on. Thanks a lot for your help and the drinks.'

'Was . . . Look, was Bert really croaked?'

'We can't be sure. But the medical evidence says he could have been. And there wasn't a suicide note.'

'Who could the lonely old sod have written one to?'

'Why not to you?'

She seemed shocked by the question.

·   ·   ·   ·   ·

Betty Morgan said, in a sweet, small-girl voice: 'I wouldn't say no to another drink just for once, sweetie.'

Morgan took her glass and went over to the cocktail cabinet, new but made in the style of traditional furniture with considerable inlay and curved ball and claw feet. He poured out a strong gin and Italian.

'Did I tell you I saw Jean this afternoon?' she asked.

'You mentioned it earlier on.' He didn't like Jean for several reasons, the most pertinent of which was that she always tried to patronize him.

'She told me about a new little dress shop that's started up in Donaldson Street. She said it's really chic.'

'I hope you didn't . . .' He stopped.

She smiled. 'You hope I didn't what, love?'

'Nothing,' he answered miserably, as he returned across the room and handed her the glass.

'She said I ought to see it, so we went along together for a quick look-see.'

He did not have to guess what was to come.

'Jean said their clothes were really nice – nothing cheap and shoddy – and she was absolutely right. There was a blue and red pleated outfit in the new line that's all the thing now and it was an absolute dream. Actually, I tried it on, but it was too small for me.' She giggled. 'The woman in the shop is a bit of a lesy and she told me I was a shade too big a girl for it. I got scared that she was going to try and hold hands.'

Girl? Had the description ever been more inappropriate?

'You'd have really liked me in it, Brian. If only it had fitted.' She spoke very casually. 'She did say she could get my size.'

'You told her to forget it? We can't afford to buy

64

anything more. You did tell her that, didn't you, Betty?'

'Come off it, love. The clothes weren't really expensive – not when you realize what they are.'

'But . . .' He went over to the cocktail cabinet and poured himself out a Scotch. 'Then is she ordering this other size?'

'I suppose she must be.'

'Can't you begin to understand . . .'

'There you go again! Why do you always have to spoil everything by getting so stuffy? What's the harm in just seeing the dress? That doesn't mean I have to buy it. And even if I did buy it, as Jean says, the best is always a bargain. . . . Come on, sweetie, smile.'

He sat. What did other husbands do in this sort of a situation? Force their wives to see financial sense? But he had never been of a masterful nature and whenever he tried to insist he was all too conscious of sounding petulant, not authoritative. . . .

'When you look all angry like that, Brian, you really scare me!'

He'd never even begun to scare her, not even when her cruelty – for she was cruel – goaded him almost (it was forever almost) beyond endurance. At times he wondered if she were a psychological masochist whose cruelty towards him was triggered by his inability to treat her with harsh contempt.

'Come over here and have a cuddle. Tell me you don't really want to frighten me.'

How ever many times before had it happened? The really absurd thing was that if only he could treat her with indifference, his abject part in the coming scene wouldn't happen.

She said, in a low, husky voice: 'I want you to be

extra nice to me because I made a very special promise to myself.' She giggled coyly. 'Do you know what I promised?'

Even as he told himself that this time he wouldn't be a fool, he crossed to the settee. She gently nibbled his ear, then trickled her lips down his right cheek. 'In your heart of hearts, you do like to see me well dressed, don't you?' She paused. 'You know, love, it's truly a lovely dress and even Jean was envious and said she wished it suited her.'

'How much is it?' he asked hoarsely.

'Just a teeny, weeny bit more than the last dress you bought me.'

He'd never been allowed to know what that had cost.

She finished her drink and put down the glass. 'If the right size really does suit me and I look as smart in it as I did in the wrong size ... You wouldn't really mind too, too much, would you?' She moved her hand up his leg. 'I'd be ever so, ever so specially grateful.'

He kissed her with a wild hunger which experience had taught him was incapable of satiation.

'My, we are all eager!'

In the bedroom she undressed with provocative casualness. Then when she was naked, she said she needed a clean nightdress but couldn't find one and kept brushing past him, evading his hands with giggling good humour.

From the moment he'd first met her, he'd been physically attracted to her with a passion that at times seemed little short of madness. It stripped him of self-control and self-respect.

She decided not to wear a nightdress after all and climbed into bed. When he joined her, she kissed him

66

and her hands caressed his body, bringing fire with their touch.

'Love,' she said, 'you will let me buy that dress as a special treat, won't you?'

He'd have granted her the world at that moment.

'I knew you would,' she whispered, her tone both complacent and contemptuous.

．　．　．　．　．

There were six lock-up garages, three on either side of the extension to the road which formed a dead-end. The nearest street light was thirty yards away and a plane tree, set in the pavement, stood between it and the garages so that even in winter they were largely in shadows.

The car stopped when the front of its bonnet was level with the two middle garages. Two men, one of them with a package in his right hand, climbed out of the car. They forced the lock of the middle left-hand garage so expertly they might have been using the key and lifted the door. The man with the package turned it upside down, then put in under the petrol tank of the Vauxhall inside. They returned to their own car and drove away.

The parish clock, half a mile away, marked the half-hours and the hours. The drizzle turned into rain. Then, at four-thirty-one, the sulphuric acid in the bottle inside the package under the Vauxhall finally ate through the cork stopper and flowed down on to a mixture of potassium chlorate and powdered sugar. The fire was immediate and violent.

9

Josephine Fusil dished the eggs and bacon and placed the two plates in front of her husband and son, Timothy, who sat at the small kitchen table.

Timothy looked curiously at her. 'Aren't you having any, Mum?'

'No. I'm on a diet.'

'Since when have you been on that?' asked Fusil.

'From the moment I weighed myself yesterday afternoon in the chemists and discovered our scales are under-reading by over half a stone.'

He smiled briefly. 'Why panic? I'd describe you as a fine figure of a woman.'

'Which is a way of telling me I'm getting fat, but you daren't come out and tell me so frankly. Coward!' She picked up the bread board and put this on the table. She was a handsome rather than a beautiful woman, largely because her face was filled with lines of character. Reserved by nature, some of the P.C.s' wives referred to her as always being pleasant to the peasants; but the truth was that she viewed rank with the same detachment as wealth or social position and like her husband she valued a person for what he or she was, not what he or she possessed.

Fusil cut open his eggs so that the yolks ran out on to the toast underneath. 'I don't know if I'll be able to get back for lunch today: we've work enough on our plates to keep us going twenty-five hours a day.'

She put in her place setting a plate with two slimming rolls on it and then sat. 'I've told you before, I'm not having you work yourself into an early grave, so you get back, even if it's only for a short time.'

He shrugged his shoulders.

'I'm playing for the Probables against the Possibles this afternoon, Dad,' said Timothy. He didn't resemble either of his parents in looks, but he did seem to have inherited their ability to make level judgements in most matters.

'Score a couple of goals. It would be great to see you in the team.'

'Old Twitchers seems to think I'll make it. The only thing is, Rog and me are really playing for the same place in the team and he's pretty good.'

'Kick him in the shin at the start of the game when the ref's not looking.'

'Bob, that's not funny!' said Josephine. 'You know I don't like you talking in that way.'

Fusil winked at Timothy. His wife had never learned to appreciate his sense of humour.

The telephone rang and Fusil started to rise. 'You stay where you are and I'll take it. My breakfast can't get cold,' said Josephine, with a quick look of distaste at the slimming rolls.

Fusil added sugar to his coffee and drank. He mopped up the last of the egg yolk on a piece of toast, added a corner of bacon, and ate. Josephine returned. 'Who is it?' he asked, his voice muffled.

'Your office. I told them you'd be along soon, but there seems to be some sort of panic on.'

He began to get up.

'I've rung off, so you can just finish your breakfast before getting back on to them: I doubt the panic will get any worse in that time. Here's the fresh toast and marmalade and do you want any more coffee?' She stared directly at him, daring him to leave until he'd finished his meal.

In just one respect, he thought sardonically, Josephine and Miss Wagner were alike – they both thought they knew best how he should run his job. As soon as he'd finished, he went out into the hall and rang the station.

'A message is in, sir, of a fire in a concrete and asbestos lock-up garage in Steerforth Road early in the morning, first reported to the fire service at four-forty-seven. By the time the fire unit arrived one of the garages and the car in it were well alight and the car's a complete write-off. The reason why the fire people have been on to us is that apparently there's a strong chance it was arson, although I can't tell you what makes 'em say that.'

'I'll be at the station in ten minutes. Get on to the fire investigation officer and arrange a meeting at the site in half an hour.'

After replacing the receiver, Fusil lifted his mackintosh and hat from the hall stand. 'I'm off,' he shouted.

'Don't you forget, I want you back here for lunch,' Josephine called back.

·   ·   ·   ·   ·

Kerr arrived at the bank at ten minutes past nine, some time after he should have started work: but since he wasn't reporting direct to the station, neither Fusil nor Campson would be able to know for sure when he had started.

The clerk at the 'Enquiries' counter used an internal phone to learn that Hanna would be free in ten minutes.

Kerr sat down at one of the small tables and picked out a leaflet from the box on it. The advantages of a bank personal loan, buy today and pay tomorrow. But detective constables didn't buy today because they were never in a position to pay tomorrow.

'Mr Hanna's free now. Will you go through?'

Hanna was tall and thin, with a deeply lined face and a craggy nose which together made him look as if he were always worried. His sandy hair was thinning and he grew it long and carefully brushed it across his skull to try and cover up his growing baldness. He came round the desk and shook hands. 'I gather you want another word with me?'

'Sorry to bother you, but there are still one or two points I need to clear up.'

'Of course. Do sit down.'

After sitting, Kerr looked at the leather photograph frame on the desk and he was, because of the positioning of the frame, just able to see the photo of a woman. She looked so angular that if he'd sat behind the desk he would have left the photo in a drawer.

Hanna waited for Kerr to speak, then became more and more fidgety when nothing was said. He cleared his throat. 'You . . . er . . . You think I can help you some more?'

'Yes, I do,' replied Kerr confidently.

'But as I said last time, I know absolutely nothing about the bank robbery.'

Kerr smiled.

'Why can't you understand? I knew where the plan of the alarm system was kept because it was my job to know, but I haven't looked at it since I first came to the branch, four years ago.'

'Are you quite sure of that?'

'I swear I haven't opened the locker in those four years.'

'But I suppose you frequently go down into the strong-room?'

'Well, of course I do. I may need one of the confidential files or books. And it's my job to check in deliveries of fresh currency and to check out loads of old currency which is going for pulping.'

'And you'll often be down there on your own?'

'I'm not the only member of the staff who goes down there alone. Any of us can . . . I tell you, I haven't touched the box in which those plans are kept in four years.'

'Tell me – have you ever been approached to give confidential information?'

'Good God, of course I haven't! . . . What I mean is, if I had I'd have reported that immediately. There's a standing rule that anything the slightest suspicious has to be reported immediately to the manager and to internal security.'

'No one's offered you a large sum of money?'

'I've just told you. Look, I've worked for this bank ever since I left school. I don't want to sound boastful but I've every chance of getting a managership soon so I just couldn't be such a fool as to throw everything away by not reporting that kind of an incident.'

'Didn't someone once say that every man has his price? They could have tried a very large bribe.'

'It wouldn't matter how large. I've a family. D'you think I'd ruin their lives as well as my own?' He spoke more excitedly. 'If it were ten thousand, twenty thousand, it wouldn't matter. I couldn't ever let my family down. My house is on a mortgage. We get special rates because I work in the bank and there's still a lot of the capital to be paid and if I did anything wrong and was sent to jail where would my family be?'

'People only get sent to jail if they're caught. Before that happens, they always think they're far too clever to be caught.'

'But I've always been too scared to do anything. I don't mean that's the only reason I've never been dishonest, but I . . .' He trailed off into silence, then said: 'You've got to understand, it's not me.'

'You know, of course, that we've checked all the accounts of everyone who works in this bank?'

'Yes, and there isn't a penny in mine which shouldn't be there: not a single penny.'

'You've no other bank or savings account which so far you've forgotten to mention?'

'I've told you about everything.'

Kerr stood. 'Well, thanks very much, Mr Hanna. I'll say good-bye, but I expect I'll be seeing you again.'

'Why won't you believe me when I tell you the truth?'

'I've never said I don't.'

Kerr was not the most modest of men and he left the bank congratulating himself on his handling of the interrogation. Not once had he made a definite accusation, yet Hanna had been left in a muck-sweat. Five years to detective inspector? Yet why not make that detective chief superintendent while he was about it? He grinned. A man should at least be ambitious.

.   .   .   .   .   .

Fusil stood by the side of Jepson, the fire investigating officer, and stared at the blackened lock-up garage at the end of Steerforth Road.

'One of the blokes on the pump unit was a real old

hand,' said Jepson. 'It was he who noticed the smoke.'

'How accurate a guide is that?'

Jepson spoke didactically. 'It entirely depends on what you mean by accurate. It is not proof in the terms a court uses, but it does give the basis for a very educated guess.'

'If you're right, what was the fire bomb made of?'

'Potassium chlorate and powdered sugar provided the base and sulphuric acid the trigger. When those three things come together, there's an instantaneous and violent fire. The bomb was set under the fuel tank of the car and when things got hot enough that blew up.'

Fusil turned up the collar of his mackintosh to keep at bay the light rain which was once more falling. This had probably been arson. But arson by the ransom mob or by the car's owner who had insured it for more than it was worth? Had the garage been locked and, if so, was the lock a simple or a complex one? Would a terrorist, probably an amateur in crime, be able to pick a lock?'

'It's becoming bloody,' said Jepson. He spoke as if he seldom swore. 'If they decide to fire an occupied building, I can't see what's to stop them. Unless you've now some idea of who they are?' He looked questioningly at Fusil.

'We haven't the beginning of a lead.'

'Then the ransom must be paid.'

'Pay it and within the month every town in the country will be threatened: villains are great plagiarists.'

'But how many people may be burned to death if it isn't paid?'

'That's the kind of question which keeps a policeman awake at nights.'

Bressett, who because he was junior and too good-natured to object loudly enough was given an unfair amount of the boring routine work to do, was trying accurately to type a T23 form when the telephone message came through. Albert Mickey's fingerprints were known and his C.R.O. file was numbered 262/M/4155.

He rang Records and asked for details of file number 262/M/4155.

Albert Mickey. Aged forty-nine, born in London. A string of arrests and convictions for minor offences: several times suspected of further minor crimes but not charged due to lack of evidence. Married to Ada Partridge eighteen years previously, separated at some unrecorded date, known to have lived for short periods with two women, for one of whom he was suspected of having pimped. No known relations (wife's address not known), no special associates.

After asking for the file to be sent on, Bressett rang off. Mickey appeared to be a small time crook who was without much imagination, perhaps old fashioned enough not to use violence. In criminal terms, a failure. So what could he have done to warrant his being murdered (if he had)?

Bressett went along the passage to the detective sergeant's room. Campson was speaking on the phone and Bressett had to wait nearly five minutes before passing over the paper on which he'd noted the details from Mickey's file.

'This isn't going to help us much,' said Campson.

'No, Sarge.'

'We've got somehow to find out what he's been up to and who he's been mixing with. Start off by seeing what his wife can tell us.'

'But her present whereabouts isn't known . . .'

'I can read,' cut in Campson curtly. 'But that's just what Records say and half the time they're too lazy to check out everything. Get on to the last address, find out where they were married, question relatives. . . . Someone will know where she's living now. Have you questioned them at the bed-sittery to discover his recent background?'

Bressett wondered whether to point out that Mickey was presumed to have no known relatives, then wisely decided not to. 'No, Sarge.'

'Why the hell not? Do I have to tell you everything you have to do and precisely how to do it?'

'There just hasn't been time. . . .'

'There's always time.'

Bressett made no answer. There was something of the bully in the detective sergeant and Bressett was not a man to stand up for himself against rank.

'All right. Get moving.'

Bressett returned to the games room. Smith was sitting behind his desk and smoking. He was thirty-four and looked more: many would describe his face as the kind from whom one would try not to buy a used car. 'Still rushing around?' he said. 'It's got like a bloody madhouse these last few days.' He had a very slight impediment of speech and slurred an occasional

word. 'If I could work a transfer back to my old div I'd
be off like a shot.' He was as cynically unambitious as
Bressett was naively ambitious. He tried to slide through
each day without exerting himself overmuch, either
physically or mentally.

Bressett went over to one of the book cases and picked
out from it a London telephone directory.

'The old man's like a bear with two sore heads. Why
doesn't someone tell him there's no bonus for collecting
a throm from overwork? My last D.I. had the right
idea: don't kill yourself working, it only makes the
pension fund smile.'

Bressett checked the number he wanted and dialled
it. He asked for details of the marriage between Albert
Mickey and Ada Partridge which had taken place
eighteen years before. He apologized and said he didn't
know either the exact date of the marriage or where the
ceremony had taken place. 'You must reckon we've
nothing much to do,' said the other man, with sarcastic
bad temper.

    .   .   .   .   .

Kerr entered the courtyard at the back of the station
as Fusil came out of the building, so he hurried to make
it clear he was not over an hour late in reporting for
work. ''Morning, sir. I'm just back from questioning
Hanna, the assistant manager at the bank.'

'Well?' Fusil's manner became curt whenever the
pressure was really on: he could not be bothered to
waste time on merely being polite.

'I'm sure there's something there, but so far I can't
pin it down. He's scared, but not scared of talking about
the robbery.'

'Has he altered any of his answers?'

77

'They're exactly the same as they were.'

A swirl of wind swept across the courtyard to flap the collar of Fusil's mackintosh against his cheek. 'We've ten times too much work in hand to spend time following up a doubtful lead in a dying case. But . . .' He was like a terrier ordered to drop a rat, but trying to get in one last shake.

'I'd say that Hanna will break if only we keep up the pressure. If I went and saw him in his own house and very obviously looked around . . .'

'I thought you were going to see him in his own place last night, not at the bank this morning?'

Kerr cursed his own over-confidence. Those had, of course, been Fusil's orders. 'I decided that it might pressure him more if I altered the venue to the bank.'

Fusil looked at him with sharp, sardonic disbelief. He then said evenly: 'I see.' It was not the first time since the amalgamation that he had relaxed his normal hard standards when dealing with one of the D.C.s who'd been in the borough force: strangely, considering his character, he allowed them a small licence he refused others. 'Then this evening you can carry out my original suggestion. In the meantime, get hold of someone from Vehicles and drive out to Steerforth Road. A car was burned out in a garage in what was probably arson. Usual enquiries.'

They parted. Fusil went over to his car and Kerr entered the building and continued through to the front room where he spoke to the duty sergeant. 'Sarge, I need help from someone in Vehicles.'

'Sorry, lad, everyone's working himself into the ground.'

'It's for Mr Fusil.'

The sergeant morosely studied Kerr.

'And he said it's top priority.'

He turned. 'Reg, you'd better put a call out for Andy to come to the front. We can spare him a bit more easily than anyone else.'

Ten minutes later, Kerr and P.C. Croft left the station in the C.I.D. Hillman, a car which had earned, but not yet been given, its retirement.

In Steerforth Road, a P.C., regulation mackintosh and helmet giving him some protection from the rain, stood watch over the lock-up garages, keeping away the few curious sightseers.

'Hullo, here come the brains,' he said, glad to have someone to talk to.

'Not forgetting the brawn!' Croft jerked his thumb in the direction of Kerr.

'And every joke guaranteed a dried-up chestnut,' said Kerr cheerfully. 'How about getting cracking, Andy, and finding out those numbers?'

'I'll need your help.'

'What? Me get my hands dirty? You're on your own, boy.'

'Bloody pansy.' Croft turned and brought out from the back of the Hillman a pair of grubby overalls which he pulled on over his uniform. He changed his shoes for wellingtons and then carried a torch into the blackened and stinking garage.

Kerr spoke to the P.C. 'Have you any idea who owns the car?'

'It's a bloke called Huggins who lives in number fifty-seven. You ought to have heard him going on about this fire – you'd have thought it was a Rolls gone west, not a Vauxhall . . . Here, you've nothing to do. Cover me whilst I nip into the car for a drag – haven't had the chance of a smoke since I came on duty.'

'Hang on a sec. The door of the garage is open – have you any idea how it was when the firemen got here?'

'A couple of feet off the ground, almost certainly to feed air to the fire. Now for God's sake stop asking questions and let me get on kissing terms with a fag.' He hurried across to the Hillman.

Kerr walked over to the garage. The roll-up-and-over door, now raised six feet, was blackened and at one point the metal had begun to melt from the heat of the fire. The lock was intact and it was obviously of good quality.

He turned his back on the car and stared out at the rain. He normally brought a light-hearted approach to his work not only because that was his nature, but also because it provided some measure of defence against the sordid, often frightening aspects of the work. But there were cases, and this was one of them, where he could no longer remain light-hearted. It was all too easy to imagine the holocaust. A crowded store, to which Helen had by chance gone shopping, the explosion followed by a violent fire which cut off all exits. . . .

'We're in luck,' called out Croft, 'so start writing.' He waited until Kerr was ready. 'Two two four six one nine MR.'

'What's that – the engine or the chassis number?'

'Engine. I'm not going to get the chassis number if I spend the next twelve hours poking around the wreck. So now let's get the hell out of here. The place is beginning to give me the willies.'

So Croft also was suffering from a too-active imagination, thought Kerr.

They left the garage and the P.C. climbed out of the car and met them in the middle of the road, just before the lock-up garages. 'I'll tell you one thing for free – it's warmer out of this flamin' wet. . . . D'you find what you were after?'

'We got half of it and that'll be enough,' replied Kerr. 'I'm on my way now to have a word with the owner.'

'Don't be surprised if he breaks down and weeps on your shoulder.'

To someone who failed to appreciate the mental stress of their work, their frequent facetiousness in matters that were serious and potentially of great danger could be both perplexing and irritating.

Huggins was a small, fat man, who spoke nineteen to the dozen. 'That car was in perfect condition. No question. I polished it every Sunday morning: if it was fine I did it outside, if it was wet in the garage. Smartest car in the road, no argument. And serviced exactly as the book says. What's more, there was over two hundred quid's worth of extras on it. And now? A wreck. Just a wreck.'

'But I suppose it was insured?' asked Kerr.

'Yes. But tell me this – are they going to pay me for all the work I did? Are they going to say it was the smartest car in the road with two hundred quids' worth of extras, so give the man a proper deal? Not them! Insurance companies are all the same. Grab your money, but never pay out properly.'

'As a matter of interest, how much was it insured for?'

'Twelve hundred quid and worth double. Think twelve hundred quid is going to buy a car as good? You've got to be joking! Why didn't the fireraisers choose the end garage, that's what I'm asking? The car there doesn't even get washed down.'

'Why d'you talk about fireraisers in the plural?'

'There were two of them, weren't there?'

'How can you be certain of that?'

'Old Ma Nesbitt said. Knows everything, does that old bitch!'

'But how could she possibly know?'

'She saw 'em. And what did she do about it? I'll tell you. She did sweet Fanny Adams, but just went back to bed, or whatever. And never heard the fire engine. Dumb old cluck.'

'Where does she live?'

'Next door.' He pointed. 'I'll tell you, there's no one can move without her peering round the curtain to see what's up.'

You never knew how a case was going to twist and turn, thought Kerr. 'May I have a look at your car papers, now, please?'

The registered number of the engine corresponded with the number Croft had discovered: there had not been a substitution of cars. 'One last thing – can you remember if you locked the garage last night?'

'Of course I locked it. D'you think I'd leave my car there for anyone to pinch? Not that locking up has done me any good, has it?'

Kerr commiserated with the small, fat man once more, then left the house and walked along the short path to the gate. As he stepped on to the pavement, Croft hurried up to him. 'Come on, let's move. I've got to be at the station . . .'

'You'll have to hang on until I've had a word with the old biddy who lives next door.'

'Just take your time and don't bother about anyone else,' said Croft bad-temperedly.

The front door of number fifty-five was opened before Kerr could press the bell-push.

'I saw you coming up the path,' said Mrs Nesbitt.

She was a thin, shapeless woman who wore even more shapeless clothes. Her face was long and narrow and above a pronouncedly hooked nose were a pair of sharp, beady, brown eyes. 'You're one of the policemen, aren't you? You went into the garage just now.'

'That's right.'

'What's that? You need to speak up a little. Everyone mumbles these days.'

She was deaf, but not prepared to admit that fact.

She showed him into a darkly furnished sitting-room which was scrupulously clean but had the dead atmosphere of not having been used in years. Shouting, he asked her if she'd seen anything in the early hours of the morning which might have to do with the fire in the garage?

She nodded and smiled, an expression which transformed her face and made it lively. 'I don't sleep much these nights: just a little doze and I wake up. Sometimes I read, sometimes I remember. When you get old, you know, you do a lot of remembering. I'm lucky, I've got lovely memories.'

Because of what Huggins had said and her appearance, he had initially identified her as the traditional elderly busybody who kept watch from behind lace curtains on everything that went on outside. But he now saw that she was a woman who had had the courage to come completely to terms with lonely old age and whose interest in other people was not of a mean, inquisitive nature, but was the warm interest of someone who still liked people even if they no longer liked her.

She sat on the large wing chair, her thin, parchment-like hands carefully folded in her lap. 'I woke up early this morning and I was thirsty so I decided to make myself a cup of tea – I have a little gas ring in the spare bedroom which saves me having to come downstairs. While I was waiting for the kettle to boil I looked out at the road because it's so interesting, even when it's empty – my husband always used to say that he'd only to see a ship and he'd imagine himself sailing away in it and when I look at the road I imagine myself going for a ride.' For a moment, her expression saddened: it had obviously been a long time since anyone had offered to take her for a drive. 'Well, I saw a car come along and go to the garages. Two men got out and opened the middle one, on the left. One of them went inside.'

'Have you any idea what sort of time this was?'

'It must have been after two o'clock because it was just before two when I decided I'd make myself the tea.'

'Were you able to see what kind of car it was?'

She shook her head. 'I'm afraid I don't know any of the cars these days.'

'Did you notice the registration number?'

'I didn't think there was any reason for trying to see what it was. I just thought these people must be friends of Mr Huggins, putting something in his garage for him.'

'What colour was the car?'

'I believe . . . I believe it was dark blue, but I wouldn't like you to think that I'm at all certain of that.'

'Could you describe the two men?'

'They were too far away. And when my kettle boiled I made the tea and I didn't bother about them any more. I'm so sorry.'

'There's no need to be. You've been a great help.'

'Have I? I'm *so* glad.'

'Tell me – do you know when the fire actually started?'

'I haven't any idea. I went to my bedroom which is

at the back of the house and although I woke up again I didn't bother to make any more tea so I didn't go back into the spare bedroom. When it was light I got up and came downstairs and saw all the people in the street and then I went out and asked what was happening and tried to tell Mr Huggins about the men and his garage, but he was very upset and called me . . . Well, some not very nice names!'

'I expect he was terribly upset over his car, Mrs Nesbitt.'

'I'm sure he was, poor man.' Her tone of voice became frosty. 'But when I was young a gentleman never spoke to a lady as he did.'

She began to tell him what life had once been like for her. She was interrupted by the ringing of the front door bell. Kerr opened the door and Croft impatiently demanded to know whether Kerr was spending the rest of the day there.

Kerr said good-bye to Mrs Nesbitt after promising to call back some time and see her again.

.   .   .   .   .

'It's Durnton, here, forensic lab. Reference Albert Mickey. The deceased had a blood-alcohol level of just under point four per cent. In popular terms that means he was probably just this side of being dead drunk: certainly he'd have been incapable of rational behaviour.

'We've checked the cord and can't really tell you anything fresh. It's a nice bit of manilla – don't often see that these days – but there's nothing peculiar about it: find us the length it was cut from, though, and we should be able to match it up. The knot used to form the loop was a running bowline which might suggest a sea background, but that's obviously open to doubt and anyway not worth much in a port. The fibres have been laid upwards for a short length and because of the way they lie in relation to the way in which the rope was fixed we can confirm that a heavy weight was hauled up over a rigid surface.

'Scrapings taken from the fingernails show no human detritus amongst the general muck so it's safe to say that he didn't claw anyone. . . . And that's about all we have for you there.

'Reference the two letters in the fire/ransom case. The same typewriter was used for both of them and it was an Olympia. We'll be able to identify the machine if you bring us in one for comparison tests. The paper is manufactured by one of the very large firms and is distributed all over the country. No individual characteristics in either sheet. The envelopes are, so far, unidentified, of poor quality. There's nothing to tell you about the postmarks, except that they haven't been tampered with.'

　　　·　　　·　　　·　　　·　　　·

Police, both uniform and C.I.D., in Fortrow and Newcastle continued to question wholesale and retail chemists and firms handling chemicals to see if they could trace unusual sales of sulphuric acid or potassium chlorate. It was a thankless task.

The conference room at county H.Q. was an elegant rectangular room with arched windows and a doorway leading out on to a balcony with intricate wrought-ironwork. There were two fireplaces, one at either end, with carved wooden mantelpieces: neither was ever used because of the amount of fuel which would have been needed.

The oval table, reproduction Regency, was large, yet in this room it appeared only of medium size. The chief constable sat at the head, near to one of the wall radiators which were hopefully believed adequately to heat the room. He was a handsome man, in his early fifties, who always dressed very smartly. His manner was courteous unless he was dealing with a fool and then it became peremptory.

He addressed Fusil, who was standing half-way along the right-hand side of the oval table. 'Boiling it all down, what you're saying is that you're more than ever convinced that we're dealing with villains, not terrorists?'

'Yes, sir.' Fusil knew that a more careful man would have hedged a bit here. 'The lock on the garage door was a fairly complex one and it was expertly picked.'

The assistant chief constable, older than the chief constable, a grizzled man with the face of a prizefighter, said in his abrupt manner: 'Why shouldn't a terrorist be capable of picking a lock.' He swung round to face Lancome. 'Eh?'

'No reason at all, sir,' answered Lancome quietly. 'They usually gen up on their subject. Look at the quality of some of the time bombs they turn out and the organization behind the political kidnappings.'

'Well, Fusil,' said the chief constable, 'can you offer us any more substantial grounds for your convictions?'

Fusil could not quite conceal his irritation. Menton's mouth tightened, but the chief constable made no comment.

'I think this might be the point . . .' began Menton ponderously.

'Just one moment,' interrupted the chief constable. He turned to Lancome. 'I'd like to hear your general thoughts before we move on.'

Fusil sat as Lancome stood. Lancome looked down briefly at the folder in front of himself, but did not open it. 'As far as proof goes, I can add nothing. In A.T. we still haven't the slightest lead on any terrorist organization calling itself O.F.S.E. As I've pointed out before, that doesn't necessarily lead to any negative conclusion.' He rubbed his long, thin nose, then pulled his finger away sharply as if he'd caught himself in an annoying mannerism. 'But I do think it would be right to see some significance in the fact that there hasn't been any propaganda: no list of aims, no diatribe against all social inequalities which are to be abolished, no ringing declarations of Utopia.' He paused, thought for a moment, then continued. 'I can remember saying that whereas the average terrorist is at great pains to disappear into the background, the average villain loves displaying himself as Mr Big. Well, the terrorist may personally want to be invisible, but he also wants to be considered an idealist and to broadcast his aims and ideals as widely as possible. This case has had a great

88

deal of publicity, yet there hasn't been a single word of propaganda.' He stopped abruptly, making them initially think that he had intended to say more.

The chief constable said: 'How much significance do you place in this?'

Lancome hesitated.

'We're not going to quote you.'

'Then, sir, I'd say that, taken in conjunction with other factors we've discussed, I would now be far more inclined to agree with Inspector Fusil than to disagree with him.'

'So do you suggest we alter the bias of our investigation?'

'I imagine, sir, that Inspector Fusil will tell us that that's not really necessary.'

They smiled, except for Menton.

'As far as A.T. are concerned, will the case still be treated as priority?' asked the chief constable

'Of course, sir.'

'Then I think we can say this. It is our present judgement, based on all known facts, that we are dealing with villains and not terrorists. Which means that this is a good moment to ask Inspector Fusil for a précis of what is happening.'

Fusil stood up once more. He could have made out that the investigations were not going too badly, but he chose to give the facts baldly, bluntly acknowledging that in practical terms no progress had been made.

Menton looked sourer than ever. Long ago he had learned that a spoonful of sugar really did help the medicine go down.

'If you've made no progress,' said the chief constable, 'you must have been asking yourself, why not?'

'Yes, sir. And one of the reasons is that until now

we've been badly hampered by the need to keep every-thing low key. But the publication of a third letter, assuming there is one, is going to panic a lot of people who've remained calm up to now and that, ironically, is going to help us. We can admit the position's nasty and ask the public to help. In this context I'd say that someone on TV explaining the situation and asking for all possible information should be our first move. Then I'd like to be able to up the grass money until it's really heavy: say five grand.'

The assistant chief constable whistled.

'Isn't that putting the sum rather high?' asked the chief constable mildly. 'We'd have a hell of a job to find that much out of ordinary funds.'

'We must offer enough to break all ordinary loyalties.'

The chief constable said slowly: 'I suppose you're right. Though I wish to God I could leave you to do the arguing with Finance.' He sighed as he wrote on the pad in front of himself.

'On top of that, sir, we must have an increase in foot patrols in Fortrow which means drafting in extra men. And when the public starts flooding in the information, I'll need at least a dozen extra hands in C.I.D.'

'See to that, John.'

The assistant chief constable made a note.

'One final thing, sir. We must have a country-wide turn-up of all villains big enough to have thought up this scheme, not just those who've dealt in arson.' He sat.

There was some coughing, a rearranging of papers, a murmured conversation. Lancome asked if he could go because he had to speak to his H.Q. As he left, the chief constable looked at his slim gold wrist-watch, given to him many years before by a woman whose life he had saved when a sergeant. 'Gentlemen, we are left with one matter to discuss. We will assume the worst which is that we fail to get a lead on these arsonists. Their threats tell us that if the ransom, on an ever-increasing scale, isn't paid, the fires will become more and more serious. Lives are threatened and it's unrealistic not to expect some, or many, to be lost. At what stage do we recommend that the ransom money, whatever it amounts to, be paid?'

'Never,' said Fusil immediately.

The chief constable looked enquiringly at him.

'If they get their money it'll be the most successful ransom job in this country. Inevitably, there'll be a rash of copy jobs until nowhere in the country will be safe.'

'I'm not going to disagree with you on that point, but obviously public disquiet will increase until we may be forced to give in, whatever the inevitable results. We have to remember that it won't be just one person's life at stake, as in a snatch, but quite possibly it will be hundreds.'

'The principle, sir, has to remain the same.'

'Principles, Fusil, can quickly become too expensive. . . . Obviously, the only real solution is to identify and smash the mob. So having assumed the worst, we'll now assume we prevent its coming to pass. Menton, you will move down to Fortrow and take charge of the investigations, personally reporting back to me. Fusil, no doubt you feel more than capable of staying in command, but in a matter this serious the most senior officer available must obviously take over.'

Fusil patently disagreed.

•   •   •   •   •   •

Fusil, back in his office in Fortrow, stared out of the window. It was unreasonable to suffer resentment because Menton had been brought in to take overall command of the investigations, nevertheless he did so. Instinct told him that sooner or later this case was going to call for the experience which came from the harsh field work where decisions had to be immediate and rules were for bending, not the experience which came from the subtle manoeuvres of administration where decisions were carefully calculated and rules were inviolate.

He turned, crossed to his desk and sat on the edge of this. One of the first questions was still no nearer being answered. Was the mob a local or an outside one? The first letter and the fact that the local grassers had come up with nothing argued for an outside mob (although outside villains were usually noted). True, the second letter had been posted locally, but then that might have been solely because the mob had had to come to Fortrow. But would a mob on a job like this, where local knowledge was so important, come in from outside? Wouldn't they choose their own home ground, where their presence would cause no comment, provided only that they'd never been connected with a torch job so that they wouldn't automatically become suspect? . . . It could be argued either way.

Had he done everything that could be done? Had he missed a single point, no matter how small?

How did one go about nailing an unknown number of men whose existence was so far only confirmed by two letters and two fires? He leaned across his desk and used the internal phone to speak to Kerr.

'That woman, Mrs Nesbitt, who said she didn't notice the registration number of the car outside the lock-up garage and couldn't guess at its make – will it do any good going back and trying to jog her memory?'

'No, sir, I'm pretty certain it won't. She mentioned her sight wasn't all that good. Even if she tried to read the letters and figures from her house, which is a fair way up the road, I don't reckon she could have done. But in fact it never occurred to her there could be any reason for trying to read them. It's not that she's soft in the head, far from it, but she's old and not bothering about the world very much so she didn't begin to think these men were doing anything suspicious. They were just friends of Mr Huggins. And as for the make of car – I doubt she could tell a Citroën from a Cadillac.'

Fusil swore. 'In any case, the car would have been nicked! Goddamn it, we're lunging around in the dark with both hands tied behind our backs.' He slid down from the desk. 'O.K. If you see Sergeant Campson, tell him I want a word with him.'

He replaced the receiver. Menton would want an office, so he'd have to come into this one. Campson would have to move out of his . . .

The external phone rang and the caller was Harvey.

'I've had another letter, Bob, postmarked London.'

Had the mob posted it on their way back up north? Or had it been posted in London further to confuse the trail? 'Are they claiming the garage fire?'

'I wouldn't know. I managed to get things organized so that the letter was picked out immediately and it's been left unopened.'

'Remind me to thank you.'

'Remind yourself to tell me what it's all about before the news goes public. . . . You understand, don't you, that if it is claiming the garage there'll be no holding back on the story? Half my staff are already on to Fleet

Street at the firm's expense, giving the story and trying to make extra line money.'

'As a matter of fact, we'll very soon be putting out a request for the press to give the facts, as gently as possible, and to ask the public for their help.'

'Give 'em as gently as you like, you're going to have a very scared public. Damnit, I keep wondering if my wife's safe. I've already been on to her three times today to find out. She probably thinks I'm having an affair with my secretary.'

'And you're not?'

'Very flattering, but regretfully I've passed the age of indiscretions.'

Fusil said good-bye. He leaned back in the chair and closed his eyes. Tiredness momentarily formed bands of colour in his eyes. What was it like to work regular hours at a job where the lives of others did not depend directly on the decisions one made?

He telephoned the duty sergeant to arrange collection of the letter from the *Gazette*'s offices, then looked through the paperwork and messages on his desk. More crimes, ranging from the ludicrous to the very serious. Inevitably, many of the cases would be only cursorily investigated so that the perpetrators had a very good chance of escaping justice. That this fact was quite beyond his control did nothing to lessen his sense of anger.

He suddenly felt hungry and remembered for the first time that not only had he not returned home to lunch, he had not even had lunch.

•   •   •   •   •

To Bressett's alarm, Mrs Prosser, who had clearly been drinking, smiled coquettishly at him as she opened the front door of her house more widely. 'Of course I remember you – such a handsome young man.'

Yet when Fusil had been with him, she had ignored him. He wished Fusil were there now. 'I'm sorry to bother you again. . . .'

'You come along into my front room and we'll have a drop of something to stop you being so serious.'

'I'm afraid it's a bit too early. . . .'

Too polite to escape the invitation, he followed her into the sitting-room, where she gave him one of the strongest gin and tonics he had ever had. For two drinks she was content merely to ogle him, but then she became impatient and she joined him on the settee, rested her hand affectionately on his thigh, and assured him that many a wonderful tune was played on an old fiddle. Bressett, certain that this fiddle had long since been played to destruction, hastily finished his drink, wriggled free of her amorous clasp, stood up, asked her who in the house would be most likely to tell him what he wanted to know, and hurriedly went out of the room. She shouted after him that as soon as he'd finished his work he must have another little drink with her. Whoever had coined the phrase about a fate worse than death, he thought, had got things wrong.

He went upstairs to the first landing. He came from the countryside and the stale air of this house, smelling of defeated lives, sickened him. He walked to the end of the corridor and knocked on the right-hand door. A tired, quavering voice answered.

Nolan could have been as old as seventy, although he claimed to be only fifty-five: his face was deeply lined, his complexion grey, his hair sparse, his teeth ill-fitting, and when he spoke he often dribbled.

'You could 'ave knocked me down with 'alf a feather,

95

and that's God's truth. Old Bert croaking hisself. And I was talking to 'im only the night before. In this room. Came in looking for a fag, like 'e often did: it's cheaper smoking other people's fags. . . .'

After a while, Bressett broke in to ask: 'What kind of a bloke was he?'

'All right, so long as you kept off football. Yell the hind legs off of a donkey, 'e would – and 'e didn't know nothing about it!'

'Did he go to matches a lot?'

'Never. Just read about 'em in the papers and watched the matches on telly, if old Ma Prosser would let 'im.' He winked: it was an obscene gesture. 'She took a shine to Bert. Used to give 'im drinks and take 'im out eating. Come back, 'e would, and tell us what all the eats was. Didn't do 'im no good, did it.'

Obviously, Mickey's relationship with Mrs Prosser had been resented by at least some of the other bed-sitters. 'Did he have much money of his own?' asked Bressett.

'Couldn't rub the shine off one halfpenny with another. Always on the bum.'

'But that can't have been because he was on the rocks, since he'd fifty-two quid in his wallet when he died.'

'Fifty-two quid! I don't believe it.'

'That's dead right.'

'The old bastard,' said Nolan, with sudden anger. 'And 'im round on a smoke cadge that night.'

'You'd no idea he'd that sort of money?'

'D'you think I'd've given 'im a smoke if I'd known? Fifty-two quid! My old woman always said I was a soft touch. I was married, once.' He stared into the distance, his eyes suddenly watering.

Bressett, very embarrassed, cleared his throat. 'Where d'you reckon the fifty-two quid came from?'

Nolan blinked rapidly. 'I wouldn't know. If I did, I'd be there, looking.'

'He never gave you any inkling of having suddenly found a source of money?'

'How's that, mister?'

'He didn't suddenly start going to the pub or smoke tailor-mades instead of rolling his own?'

'Weren't never anything but on the bum. . . . Mister, Ma Prosser's been saying maybe Bert didn't croak himself, but got croaked?'

'We can't be sure yet, but he may have been murdered.'

He mumbled something and looked scared.

'As far as you knew, then, he didn't have any money?'

'That's right.'

'Did he ever talk to you about what he did when he went out? You know the kind of thing – the people he met and where he'd been?'

'Never nothing like that. Bert didn't do much talking.'

'Did he ever say where he'd come from before he lived here?'

'Never heard him mention anything 'cept he liked London a lot more'n Fortrow and wished 'e was back.'

'How long ago was it that he lived in London?'

'Never 'eard.'

'He died late Tuesday night or early Wednesday morning. Did you hear anything during the night, like people moving about or coming up or going down the stairs?'

Nolan shook his head.

'You must have talked about all this to the others in the place – did anyone hear anything suspicious?'

'Nobody 'eard nothing, not even Andy who says he don't ever sleep, but then 'e's as deaf as a post.'

'Did he go out any time Tuesday evening?'

'Yeah, after cadging a smoke – and him with fifty-two quid in his pockets!'

'Did he say where he was going?'

'No.'

'What time was this?'

Nolan shrugged his shoulders. 'It were after dark.' Time did not have much relevance for him.

Bressett checked his notebook, put that in his coat pocket, and stood. 'If you think of anything else, give us a ring at the station, will you?'

He went downstairs. As he stepped off the last stair, Mrs Prosser opened the door of her sitting-room. 'There you are! I've been waiting and waiting. Come and have that little drinkie.'

'My detective inspector. . . . Frightfully sorry. . . .' He hurried across to the front door. Pray God the other blokes at the station never heard how he'd had to run to save his honour.

.   .   .   .   .

The letter, still dusty from the dark powder which Detective Sergeant Walsh had brushed all over the envelope, was brought up to Fusil by a P.C. He read the very brief message. 'You're now in for two million and that's all right by us. Get that message on to the front page of the *Gazette* or it'll be four million. And next time someone may get all burned up about it.'

He slammed his clenched fist down on to the desk.

12

It was trite to say that large events hinged on small happenings, but it was true. If on Friday Helen had not gone to spend the evening with her parents at Farnleigh, if Kerr had not been so late in leaving the station it had not been worth bussing to Farnleigh, if Hanna had not lived close to the bus route from the station to Kerr's house . . . But Helen had gone to Farnleigh, Kerr didn't leave the station until eight-forty, and Hanna's house was only five minutes' walk from the bus stop outside the Chinese take-away food shop.

The woman who opened the door of Hanna's house to the extent of a chain had a high, sharp voice. 'Who are you and what do you want?'

A bit of a welcome for a start, thought Kerr. He identified himself.

'Let me see your warrant card.'

He handed this in. After a short while, the door was shut and he heard the chain being released. The door was then opened fully. The photograph on Hanna's desk had not done his wife real justice: she was twice as sternly angular in real life. Oliver Twist would never have dared ask *her* for more.

'It is inconsiderate of you to call at this time,' she informed him. 'My husband likes to spend his evenings in peace.'

And obviously the only way he'd be able to do that

would be to keep his mouth tight shut. 'May I have a word with him?'

'What is it about?'

'I have some questions I want to ask him.'

'Questions about what?'

'I think it's best to leave that until I speak to him.'

She looked at him with cold dislike, then reluctantly showed him into the sitting-room. There was a large fire of smokeless fuel and the room was warm. The television was on. The furniture was not luxurious, but it was attractive and every piece had the look of being exactly in its right and proper place.

Hanna stood up and his expression was first one of astonishment, then one of uneasiness.

'Sorry to bust in on you at this time of night,' said Kerr, with a breeziness undiminished by his reception, 'but there just hasn't been time before now to get to have a word with you. We're over the tops of our eyebrows in work.'

'I told Mr Kerr that it was most inconvenient, but he insisted on speaking to you,' said Mrs Hanna.

Hanna looked from Kerr to his wife, then back again at Kerr and belatedly he realized Kerr was still standing. 'Do sit down. Come over here where it's warm.' He stood up in a flurry and as a result half knocked over an occasional table, only just catching it in time. He cleared his throat, then said: 'There's nothing more I can tell you, you know.'

'Nothing more about what?' demanded his wife.

'About the bank robbery, dear.' He turned to face Kerr. 'That's what you've come about, isn't it?'

Kerr settled back in the chair. 'That, among other things.'

'Other things? But what else . . . Look, I never

100

touched those plans, nor have I ever spoken to anyone outside about them. Even Enid doesn't know where they're kept: in fact, she didn't know they existed.'

'I should hope not,' she snapped. 'Steven is well aware of where his duty lies.'

Rule, Britannia! 'Someone passed the news on to the people who did the job.'

'I didn't.'

'Perhaps you've an idea who did?'

'Good God, no! If I did, I'd have said so long before now. When the police made their suspicions clear the manager asked me if any of the staff suspected anything. I spoke to several people who can be trusted implicitly and not one of them has the slightest suspicion of any member of the staff. So you see.'

'I see what?'

'Well – that I can't possibly help you.'

'That doesn't follow, does it?'

'But . . . If I don't know . . . I mean, what . . .'

His wife interrupted his stumbling words. 'If my husband says he cannot help you, that's an end to it'. She looked icily at Kerr, daring him to pursue the matter.

What was worrying Hanna sick? wondered Kerr. So far, there hadn't been a hint of what it could be.

'There's nothing more,' said Hanna, trying to sound definite.

'Well . . .' Kerr let his voice die away.

'This is becoming ridiculous,' snapped Mrs Hanna.

Kerr looked directly at her. 'I'm afraid that what we have to talk about now is very confidential.'

'I do not understand what you are trying to say.'

'As you yourself implied earlier, some professional secrets have to be kept even from a wife. So if you wouldn't mind leaving the room?'

'If I'd do what?'

'Leave the room, please?'

She did not move so he stood up, crossed the floor and opened the door. He smiled cheerfully as, perhaps wondering how she had for once lost control of a situation, she walked out.

Back by the chair, Kerr took off his mackintosh and folded it on his lap, making it obvious that he was prepared to stay for as long as was necessary. He brought out a pack of cigarettes and offered this and although Hanna initially refused, he immediately changed his mind and accepted one.

Kerr settled back in the chair as he remembered one of Sergeant Braddon's favourite sayings: 'There's times when silence is worth a whole chapter of words.'

'You . . . you said you wanted to talk about something else?' said Hanna, his voice croaky.

Kerr nodded.

'Nothing that I . . . Nothing I can tell you can possibly have anything to do with the bank robbery. I swear to that.'

'I'm afraid you'll have to leave us to be the judges of that.'

'But if I promise on my oath that it's unconnected . . . ?'

'I'd believe you every time, of course. But my seniors are very suspicious people.'

'Oh, my God!' mumbled Hanna.

Kerr spoke in a brisk, chatty tone. 'Why not spit it out and get it over and done with. Things will be so much easier afterwards.'

His voice dropped to a loud whisper. 'If Enid ever learned . . .'

'Why should she? As far as she need ever know, we're

discussing a suspicion you have regarding the robbery which until now you've not dared tell anyone about because it's potential dynamite.'

Hanna drew on the cigarette, went to speak, stopped himself, and drew on the cigarette again. A couple of minutes passed during which his expression accurately portrayed the turmoil in his mind. He suddenly drew in his breath, like a man about to start on some hard, dangerous act, then said hoarsely: 'It's only occasionally. And then it's just because . . .' He ran his tongue along his lips as he looked at the door. 'She's never understood, but sometimes a man just has to.'

You poor old bastard, thought Kerr compassionately. He tried to make things easier for Hanna. 'What's her name?'

It took Hanna three attempts before he managed to say, 'Peggy.'

'Is she nice?'

Hanna was clearly disconcerted by the question. 'But don't you understand, she's a whore?'

'Yeah, of course. But I've met a lot of 'em and some are nice enough. Of course, the old story that they've hearts of gold is all cobblers. Their hearts are in their purses. Was she very pricey?'

Hanna experienced a sudden dislike for the detective. He'd managed to convince himself that the relationship had been more than just a sordid transaction, but Kerr's words had stripped away that deceit.

'How much does she charge?'

'Ten pounds,' he muttered sullenly.

'And how often d'you see her?'

'Not very often.'

'What's that mean? Twice a week?'

'Maybe . . . maybe twice a month.'

'And it's always Peggy?'

'Yes.'

'Where's she hang out?'

'In a house in Roehampton Road.'

'What number?'

'You're surely not going to see her? I've not done anything illegal . . . I don't . . .' He realized that in his excitement his voice had risen and he looked at the door with guilty fright.

'I have to check. And when I do and everything turns out exactly as you're saying, then I walk away and forget the whole matter.'

'It . . . it won't get into the papers?'

Kerr managed not to smile at the naive assumption that an assistant bank manager's visits to a prostitute were news. 'You've no need to worry about that.'

'And what about my wife?'

'She won't hear anything about it from me.'

Hanna's relief was immediate but, ironically, so was his fresh resentment that Kerr had not only learned his secret, but had also destroyed his illusions concerning it.

Kerr stood up. 'I'll be off, but before I go there's just one last thing you haven't mentioned – the number of the house in Roehampton Road?'

'Fourteen.'

As Kerr, followed by Hanna, reached the front door, Mrs Hanna came into the hall from the kitchen. 'Have you finished discussing your confidential business?' she demanded, with cold belligerence.

'Yes, we have,' Kerr answered. 'Sorry I had to ask you to leave, but you'll understand that with a bank concerned some matters are so delicate that . . . Well, they just have to be kept secret from the layman.'

She nodded distantly.

He left. Fancy having to scuttle along every now and then because his wife just wouldn't give it to him! How in the hell did a man come to marry a woman like that?

．　　　．　　　．　　　．　　　．

Saturday morning brought high winds and black-bellied clouds which promised heavy rain: it wasn't really cold, yet the dampness made it seem so.

Menton, who'd arrived in Fortrow the previous evening, was in Fusil's office and Fusil had had to move into Campson's. Fusil was a man who liked familiar things around him when working: this change to a strange room unsettled and irritated him.

Kerr reported at eight-thirty-seven. 'You're late,' snapped Fusil.

Kerr said, aggrieved since by his own standards he was early: 'The bus was held up, sir, by roadworks.' This excuse was received with scorn.

'Well? What is it?'

'I questioned Hanna last night. His trouble is that he's seeing a Tom and is scared stiff his wife will find this out.'

'What's she been charging?'

'He said it was ten quid a throw.'

'Was it?'

'I haven't checked that point yet.'

'Why not?'

'There just hasn't been time. . . .'

'There would have been if you could bring yourself to get to work before the middle of the morning. Find out what he did pay her.'

Kerr left.

Fusil tilted back his chair. Another marriage that had

a rotten core to it. There were times when he came close to believing that every human relationsip was rotten at the core, that the fight between good and evil had been won by the devil at the moment when he was cast out of heaven. At such times it was his own marriage, warm to the core, which restored to him a sense of proportion.

He picked up the copy of the *Daily Express* which he had brought with him. 'Ransom town threatened again.' He put the paper down. Publicity was usually a double-edged weapon: in this case it might help, but it was also certainly going to hurt.

There was a knock and a P.C. came in to hand him a memorandum from Menton. There was to be a conference at ten in the detective chief superintendent's room to be attended by the D.C.S., Div. S., D.C.I., and Div. I. There was to be a press conference, to be held in the parade room, at eleven, to be attended by D.C.S. and D.I.

Bloody memoranda! Now that Menton was in command they'd fly around like snowflakes in a blizzard. A case like this wasn't solved by memoranda, but by pounding the pavements, pressuring, questioning. . . . But the pavements were being pounded, the known arsonists all over the country were being pressured, as were all the villains considered capable of setting up the job, and grassers were being endlessly questioning. . . .

Had they missed anything? Goddamn it, there'd been two fires. There must be a lead somewhere. . . . A barn of hay had burned out. No one had seen the arsonist, no strangers had been noticed in the neighbourhood, no parked cars had been marked down. A garage had been burned out. An old lady, not quite with the world any longer, had seen two men but couldn't describe them, she had seen a car but had no idea what

106

make it was or what was its registration number. The second fire had probably been started by a fire bomb made up from sulphuric acid, potassium chlorate, and powdered sugar: the purchase of any of these ingredients would hardly ever cause sufficient interest to be remembered. . . .

.   .   .   .   .

All over the country teams of detectives questioned men whose names appeared in files whose numbers had been punched out by the computer. In the criminal world they were the Mr Bigs, the men who had proved their ability to organize and carry out sizable operations.

Allport was questioned by two men. The detective sergeant was neat, both in features and clothing, whilst the detective constable was a shambling bear of a man who might have been living for weeks in what he wore.

'We're always interested in you,' said the detective sergeant.

Allport smiled at them across the sitting-room of his house. 'You want to make quite certain I don't get into any trouble?'

'I couldn't put it neater.'

'Then I'll tell you, sport, and put your minds at rest. I'm busy at work, I'm fit, and I'm thirty-four next week.'

'How about inviting us to the party?'

'No one more welcome, you know that.'

'You're too kind.' The detective sergeant's manner sharpened. 'Have you been busy lately?'

'Busy all the time. I'm working with my brother-in-law who's got a small factory which makes wrought-iron wriggles for the suburban trade. Very, very profitable, though personally I wouldn't be seen dead with half the stuff.'

'Glad to hear you're a man of taste. Tell me, have you been down to Fortrow recently?'

'Now as a matter of fact, yeah, I have. Me and Janey went for the day a couple of weeks back to see some friends. Funny people, those friends. Kind of made us wonder if we were really welcome.'

'Must have been a very unusual feeling.'

'That's right, sport, it was.'

'Have you been to Fortrow since?'

'No reason for going there again, not with them acting like that.'

'So where were you this Tuesday night?'

'Where? Right here, of course, watching the telly with Janey.'

'And Thursday night?'

'No different. I've become domesticated. Just give me a warm fire, the telly, Janey, and I'm content.'

'You've become a bigger liar than ever. You were seen in Fortrow last Thursday.'

'Must have been someone else who's handsome.' Allport laughed easily. 'Come to think of it, there's a bit of a coincidence! A bloke I know has just had the splits telling him *he* was seen in Fortrow those two days – and he ain't been near the place in years. . . . What's the matter, sport? Got trouble and you don't know who started it so you're trying everyone?'

'Maybe,' agreed the detective sergeant, unperturbed.

. . . . .

Menton possessed the qualities of a good P.R. man. He faced the two TV teams and the many reporters and he spoke in a series of clichés and platitudes and managed to sound as if he were taking everyone fully into his confidence. The journalists admired his performance, while not accepting it. 'But in fact have the police really made any progress whatsoever in the case?' asked a ginger-haired woman who looked as if she'd invented women's lib.

'Let me say this. Off the record – and I stress that – we're making considerable progress. Don't forget, we've had two fires and three ransom letters. Now you'll all know that no crime has ever been committed without traces being left behind. Sometimes the traces are obvious and are easily read, sometimes they're very well hidden and call for a trained scientific team to do the reading. Here, we've been lucky – we have many of the finest forensic scientists in the country working for us.'

'So what have they found out?' asked a man with very long black hair.

Menton smiled. 'You really can't ask me to be that specific. In an investigation of this nature we have to play the cards very close to our chests or the other side will know how the game's going.' He paused and his voice deepened. 'On second thoughts, that was an unfortunate choice of words because out of context they might make it seem as if we're not taking this case as seriously as we should. Let me reassure you, we're taking it very, very seriously indeed. We've already drafted in thirty-five men from other divisions and another twenty are due tomorrow.'

'Suppose you can't identify the arson gang – will the ransom be paid?' asked a member of one of the TV teams.

'When I was a young D.C., I once said to my D.I.,

109

"Suppose such-and-such happens . . ." He tore me off a right, royal strip. "Suppose you do your adjectival job properly and then you won't need to do any adjectival supposing. . . ." So to answer your question, sir, I will suppose no such thing because the contingency will not arise.'

It was a practised performance.

13

Four extra telephone lines had been rigged up and these were brought through to the old games room which was now the local operations room. Any call from the public concerning the fires or ransom demand was routed to this room where one of four D.C.s answered it. Their brief was simple. Calm the caller, assure him or her that everything was in hand, carefully note down whatever information was given, pass that information back to a collator.

The two collators were detective sergeants. Their job was definable, yet the execution of it was partially indefinable. They had not only to note and cross-check information, but also to try to judge whether the information was both accurate and honest and here there was need for an indefinable play between instinct, experience, and common sense.

Definite, pertinent statements of fact were investigated as soon as possible. 'Look, I live in Anywhere Road and last night I saw my neighbour pouring liquid from a petrol can into a bottle. Isn't that how Molotov cocktails are made? . . .' The neighbour was visited by a policeman and in the nicest possible way he was asked to explain what he had been doing. Any generalized allegation was noted and filed, but probably not immediately investigated. 'I live next to a bloke who's always messing about with chemicals. The papers keep saying the blackmailers are probably using chemicals to start the fires and I just wondered . . .' The obvious cranks were given short shrift. 'It's punishment for our sins. The Lord is going to root out evil with the sword of fire. . . .'

The volume of calls increased until it threatened to overwhelm the running of the operations room: to the men who answered them it seemed as if a phone couldn't be on its cradle for thirty seconds before it began to ring once more.

Men and women, from the lowest ranks to the highest, worked their shifts and then carried on, careless about time as they struggled to identify their quarry.

And men in high office debated the agonizing question – at what moment in time would the threat become so deadly that the ransom would have to be paid?

.   .   .   .   .

His mood resentful, Kerr walked briskly along the well-lit pavement past large Victorian and Edwardian houses which had all been converted into either offices or flats. He'd wanted to stay on at the station, working with the others, but Fusil had told him to interview 'Peggy' and when he'd queried the reasonableness of wasting more time on that case, Fusil had torn him off a hell of a strip for insubordination. The D.I.'s main fault, he thought, was that he couldn't let go of a case which had defeated him, not even when something more important came to hand. So Hanna had visited a Tom from time to time . . . Did the identity of the traitor at the bank now matter a fig when a mob were threatening mass murder?

Number fourteen was a huge pile of a building,

looking oppressive in the shadows cast by the street lighting, as if behind its walls there worked faceless people who believed in states, not individuals. Inside the large porch, however, this suggestion was seen to be false because the two rows of buttons and name cards spoke of the lonely world of bachelor flats, not the inhumanly cold world of the bureaucrat.

He checked the name cards and then pressed the push to number five – Peggy Lea. A woman's voice asked through the grill: 'Who is it?'

'Hi, Peggy. Are you free?'

There was a buzz from behind the stout front door and when he pushed, it opened. There was a long hall, lit by an unshaded light, with four doors along its length and near the end a beautifully proportioned staircase which curled round to the right.

Number five was on the first floor. He rang the bell and a blonde, dressed in a frock which was interesting without being too obvious, opened the door. She studied him. 'I don't know you.'

'We can't be lucky all the time.'

She summed him up with professional skill. 'I'm busy. Find someone else. . . .'

'C.I.D.' He stepped inside.

She called him several unladylike names.

They stood in a large room which was bedroom to the right and sitting-room to the left. Two doors led off this and one of them gave access to a tiny kitchen.

'What the hell d'you want?' she demanded.

She looked young and yet she looked old. Twenty-one or two, he finally guessed. If she toned down the make-up she might pass as reasonably innocent, provided only that she remembered to keep smiling and didn't let her mouth draw into a hard, straight line.

'You've no right to come busting in.'

'Me bust in? You invited me.' When he'd first started work he'd felt sorry for all prostitutes, seeing them in the traditional light of women forced by financial circumstances into a sordid occupation. But experience had taught him that there were almost as many motives for turning prostitute as there were prostitutes and some of these motives allowed very little room for sympathy.

She walked over to a battered occasional table and picked out a cigarette from a brass box. She lit the cigarette and went over to the single armchair and slumped down in it. 'I've not done anything.'

'Relax. I've only come for some information. D'you recognize the name of Steven Hanna?'

'What if I do?'

'How much d'you know about him?'

'He's a friend. That's all.'

'Is he a good payer?'

'What d'you mean?'

'Does he pay you well for entertaining him?'

'Who the hell d'you think I am?'

Kerr grinned. 'How much, how often, and since when?'

She swore, then stubbed out the cigarette in an ashtray that was already half full. 'He's feeble,' she said contemptuously. 'When they were handing out backbones he got in the wrong queue.'

'If you'd ever met his wife, you'd be more charitable.'

'You have?'

'Took me two hours to thaw out afterwards.'

'He says she's a real bitch. All the marrieds talk like that.'

'In his case it's the understatement of the year.'

She lit another cigarette.

'Is he a regular punter?'

'You could call him that.'

'So how often does he come a-punting?'

She shrugged her shoulders. 'Twice a month, maybe. Not up to any more,' she added spitefully.

'And what's he pay?'

She was silent.

'Come on, don't be bashful.'

'Ten quid.'

'For the two visits?'

'Do you mind?' she said, with sudden anger. 'I'm not a bloody back-street scrubber.'

'So he's paying you twenty quid most months?'

She nodded.

Five pounds a week was surely not enough to have turned Hanna into a traitor? Or had he escaped from his wife the previous night and phoned Peggy to tell her what her answers must be? 'Most blokes with a frozen shark of a wife would want to visit someone as pretty as you much more often than twice a month.'

'There's no call to be bloody sarky.'

'Sarky? If it weren't that I've only been married for a short time . . .' He did not finish. The implied compliment was crude, but he'd never met a Tom who could resist a compliment. 'Are you sure it's been only twice a month?'

'He said he couldn't afford to visit any more. But if you ask me, two's his limit.'

'Would I be right in thinking he's a bit of a masochist?'

'He's straight.' She spoke with professional pride. 'If he weren't, it'd be more than ten quid.'

She sounded truthful, but life must have taught her to lie convincingly. That this was so was proved after a buzzer sounded. She looked at him.

'Tell him you're busy.'

'Aren't you ever bloody well moving?' She stood up, crossed to the small wall microphone, asked who the caller was, and said that she'd only just got back from shopping and must have a bath and would he call back in half an hour's time. She returned to her chair.

'I hope you don't have to put him off a second time,' said Kerr.

'I've nothing more to say to you. Why won't you go?'

'I will, just as soon as I'm convinced there really is nothing more you can tell me.' He stretched out his legs towards the gas fire and settled more deeply into the chair.

She told him what she thought of the law, the police force, and people who stopped an honest girl from working.

He smiled cheerfully.

'For God's sake, mister, clear out and leave me. I don't know nothing more about him, I swear I don't.' She spoke with resentful hopelessness If he decided to stay because he thought she was holding back information, the whole of the rest of the evening would be ruined and in just over an hour she was expecting a customer who paid her very much more than ten pounds for a visit. She stood up, stubbed out the cigarette, went over to a small sideboard and brought out a bottle of gin. 'D'you want a drink?'

'I've never been known to refuse.'

'I'll bet.' She poured out two drinks, handed him a glass. She drank quickly. 'Look, mister, if I . . .' She stopped and stared at him. 'Suppose I tell you something interesting, will you clear out then?'

'It's to do with Hanna?'

'No.'

He shrugged his shoulders.

'Mister, I keep telling you, I don't know nothing more about him. But I want you out. So if I tell you this, will you go?'

He had become convinced that she was telling the truth and therefore there was nothing to be lost by accepting her offer. 'O.K., I'm listening.'

'There's been a bloke in Ribstowe who's supposed to have croaked himself. I was talking to a friend and he said the bloke didn't croak himself, he was croaked because he was trying to black somebody big.'

'Who's the big man?'

'I don't know.'

'What's your friend's name?'

She shook her head. 'If he knew I'd grassed, he'd work me over until I wouldn't recognize myself.'

     ·   ·   ·   ·   ·   ·

'Mickey was blacking, was he?' said Fusil. He looked across the desk which was strewn with the morning's mail and crime reports. 'Who was he blacking and why and who told her?'

'She swears she doesn't know any of the answers and she won't name who told her because he'll carve her up if he ever learns she's talked to us.'

Fusil scrumpled up a circular and threw it at the wastepaper basket: he missed. The phone rang and the message was brief. He yawned, ran his right hand over his hair in a gesture of tiredness, and then said: 'Mickey was a small-time crook, a layabout cadging from his mates and his landlady. So would a man like him ever get mixed up in something strong enough to warrant his being rubbed out?'

'He did have all that money on him and normally he was skint.'

'Fifty-two quid doesn't make for much of a black, does it?'

'Maybe he didn't realize how big the job was.'

Fusil scratched the side of his face, screwing up his mouth as he did so. 'Or maybe the Tom got rid of you the easiest way she could think of.'

'I naturally wondered about that at the time, but I decided she was giving it to me straight.'

Fusil had learned to accept Kerr's judgements – or at least those which didn't contradict his own. 'O.K. Start digging. Trace out who he could have been trying to black – check back on past criminal associates – and look for more money. If the blacking was strong enough for Mickey to be killed, then surely he must have known it was big and wouldn't have settled for a mere fifty-two quid?'

Kerr hesitated. 'It'll keep a bit, won't it, until I've given a hand in the ops room?'

'Is that a discreet way of volunteering to do some extra work on a Sunday?'

Kerr grinned. 'I reckon it must be.'

'God knows, then, things must be desperate!'

.   .   .   .   .

The house was one of fifteen, erected ten years before in a close. Built partially on the open plan, it had large picture windows, double-glazed, in the main rooms. The front door was set in a fussy pretentious porch which spoiled the otherwise simple lines. The front garden was down to lawn and a gravel path went round the integral garage to the back garden. Beyond stretched fields, now almost all arable because in the past the farmers had found too many of their cattle or sheep maimed by shot or even arrows.

The three men parked the car at the end of the road which led into the close. It was a dark night and the street lighting was poor so that they were unworried by the fear that a chance encounter might lead to one or more of them being observed. They chose number one, Hatton Close, solely because it was the first house they came to. The owner could never have foreseen that the chance which led him to buy that house and not number seven was going to prove so tragic.

They crossed the front lawn: the leading man carried two plastic containers filled with petrol, the second man two parcels which he was at great pains to keep upright, and the last man a sawn-off shotgun.

The man with the containers put these down in the porch and took from his coat pocket a number of skeleton keys which looked like double-ended dentist's picks. The fourth key forced the lock. When he turned the handle, the door opened. They were in luck. The occupants had not bothered to bolt the door as well as to lock it.

They emptied one container of petrol over the bottom six feet of the stairs, the hall carpet, and the sitting-room. One of the small parcels was turned upside down and left in the corner of the petrol soaked settee. They went through to the kitchen and emptied the second container of petrol in there, making certain all the pine-wood units were well soaked. The second parcel, turned upside down, was placed under the table, with a carpet from the dining area heaped up around it.

When they left the house they relocked the front door and, as a refinement that was brutal, jammed a thin length of metal into the lock so that it could not readily be opened, even from the inside.

Four people slept in the house: husband and wife in the large bedroom at the front, daughter next to the bathroom, and son in the back bedroom. They were all sound sleepers.

The two cork stoppers had been very thin and the first one was pierced by the acid within twenty minutes of the intruders' leaving, the second one less than a minute later. There was no crashing explosion, despite the petrol fumes, but one second the hall and sitting-room were in darkness, the next they were engulfed in flame: a minute later, the kitchen was the same.

Glass shattered, wood away from the actual flames caught fire, materials curled up and were skeletonized, a small collection of toy soldiers melted and the martial figures first drooped and then collapsed, like wounded troops, the television tube imploded, wallpaper charred in seconds, rubber hosing and electrical cable disintegrated.

The mother awoke, instantly aware that something was wrong – twelve years of motherhood had sharpened her instincts – but at first not able to identify what. She heard a roaring, booming sound, puzzled over this . . . And then smelled smoke.

'David,' she screamed. She switched on the bedside lamp, but it didn't work because the main cable leading into a meter had already burned through.

'What is it? . . . What's up?' he mumbled.

She ripped back the bedclothes, and reached across for the torch which she always kept by the bed. With this switched on, she could see thick tendrils of smoke curling up from beneath the door. 'Oh Christ, David! Look!'

He leapt out of bed, ran to the door, and wrenched this open.

Flames, softened by the curling smoke, hurled up the staircase which met the landing between the bathroom and back bedroom. The scalding heat made him recoil instinctively and the smoke started a fit of coughing.

'We've got to get the children,' she cried wildly.

He had never considered himself either a man of decision or a man of much courage, but in the next few minutes he showed sharp decision and high courage. 'Open the window and get out: use a sheet to climb down.' She started to shout something, but he ignored her, stepped out into the passage, and slammed the door shut.

He pressed a handkerchief against his nose. He was terrified, but he went forward towards the appalling heat and the flames.

He slammed open the door of the nearer bedroom, which was then sufficiently illuminated for him to see that Sandra was still asleep, her face turned towards the door: her hair, which she was now growing long, trailed across one plump cheek. He dragged the bedclothes back and pulled her out of bed and she was still not fully awake when he had her cradled in his arms, although she whimpered with a growing, as yet instinctive, fright. He went through the doorway on to the landing. The heat had become fiercer, the flames more threatening, even in the last few seconds. He smelled the acrid scent of singeing hair, little realizing it was his own which burned. Sandra began to scream and wriggle and he had to hold her very tightly against himself as he ran.

His wife had knotted two sheets together and made

one end fast to a bed and she now stood by the opened window. 'Get her out,' he panted.

'What about Basil?'

'I'm going now.'

He went back out of the room to discover that there was now a barrier of fire by the stairs.

He ran towards the flames, thinking to break through them to the bedroom beyond, but the agony of the heat was too great. Sobbing, he retreated, his exposed skin already feeling painfully taut and the smell of singed hair very much stronger.

In the bedroom his wife had tied the free end of the sheet around Sandra's waist and was helping Sandra to climb over the window-sill. He grabbed one of the blankets from the bed and returned to the passage. Draping the blanket over his head and shoulders, he once more tried to force his way through the flames.

Later, he was to curse himself for not daring those final feet, he was to know the agony of wondering whether he could have made it if he'd forced himself on through the raging hell. But at the time he knew only that it was impossible.

His wife was shouting out to Sandra to go next door and wake the Calcotts and tell them to call the fire brigade. She turned. 'Where's Basil?'

'I can't get through inside. I'll have to get into the room from outside – there's the ladder in the shed.' He helped her climb out of the window and as he did so the roar of the fire grew. She reached the ground and he went over the sill and scrambled his way down, hitting his hip heavily on a downpipe but knowing nothing about this until later.

He ran round to the back garden and the toolshed. It was locked because there had been several recent cases of local vandalism and the key was back in the kitchen. Shouting wildly, meaninglessly, he struggled to break in the door, then he picked up a rock and smashed the window.

The extendable ladder was up on the roof rafters and without the door being open it was a difficult struggle to get it down, but he finally succeeded. He pushed it through the broken window.

He placed the ladder, extended, against the wall beneath the back bedroom window and climbed up. As he reached the top, the glass of the window shattered and flames leapt out, missing him only because they were sucked upwards. No one inside could still be alive.

14

Fusil stared at number one, Hatton Close. From ground level outside one saw shattered windows and smoke-stained brickwork, but that was all. Yet a twelve-year-old boy had been burned to death inside.

Basil had been one year older than Timothy. What if he were looking at his own home, knowing it was Timothy's grave . . .

'What a bastard!' said the assistant fire investigating officer, a tall redhead who had the look of a basset hound about him. 'The kid never had a chance because the place went up like a rocket.'

'So was it arson?'

He hunched his shoulders to raise the collar of his mackintosh higher. 'A sudden, violent fire, probably with two seats, very thick, acrid smoke . . . There can't be much doubt.'

'When will you know for certain?'

'Maybe when we can get inside. But I reckon you can take it now that it was firebombs and petrol. One of the troubles will be that petrol doesn't normally leave any traces unless there's an unburned edge formation around the place where it was sprinkled.' He suddenly slammed his right fist into the palm of his left hand. 'Didn't the bastards give a damn that there was a kid of twelve inside?'

A child's life meant nothing to them when it was

stacked up against millions, thought Fusil with fierce hatred.

'Are you getting anywhere in identifying them?'

'Not so far. Every bloody lead finishes in a dead end.'

'Then the money's got to be paid.'

Fusil was silent. Now they were eyeball to eyeball with the impossible dilemma which always faced the law when men without pity blackmailed it.

Two hoses had been used to cool down the interior of the house and now one of these was turned off. A fireman climbed over the window-sill of the sitting-room and they watched him as he carefully picked his way over the burned-out rubble.

'How long after the fires have the letters been arriving?' asked the assistant fire investigating officer.

'It's always been the following afternoon.'

'So there could be one this afternoon?'

'Probably.'

'Can't you trace them back?'

'Cheap mass-produced paper and envelopes. They're sold all over the country. The same typewriter, an Olympia, typed all three, but that's useless information until one has a machine for comparison tests. Postmarks were Newcastle, Fortrow, and London: if there's a meaningful pattern there I can't see it, unless it's the obvious, negative one of using different places to prevent pinpointing any one.'

'Someone outside the mob must know who they are.'

'There's five thousand on offer for the first grasser to come in with hard news: most grassers would sell their sisters into a harem for half that. So the fact there hasn't been a useful whisper means we're up against a mob with really tight security who probably haven't ever before pulled a job remotely like this one.'

'Didn't anyone see them setting fire to the place?'

'Door to door questioning is going on now, but I wouldn't give a tinker's spit for the chances of learning anything really useful.' With that last sentence, his voice expressed all the angry, bitter frustration which he was experiencing.

．　　　．　　　．　　　．　　　．

To many, D.C. Smith seemed a man who could look on tragedy without any emotion other, perhaps, than a faint curiosity. But this was an entirely false picture. When young he'd been brought up by foster parents who'd believed that children were possessed of a devil who could only be driven forth by harsh discipline and so he had learned to keep his emotions very well hidden: a habit which had never left him.

He spoke quietly to the couple who lived in number twelve, Hatton Close. 'Were you awake at all during the first part of the night?'

The husband answered first. 'I don't know about Pam, but I did wake up once. I checked the time, saw it was half two and just turned over and went back to sleep.'

'And you, madam?'

'I slept through until the fire engine arrived. Then we both got up and looked out. The Roskills' place was in flames. God, it was awful!'

'Who was outside in the street when you first looked?'

'There were just a few people by the front garden. David and Evelyn were running backwards and forwards . . .' She moved close to her husband, seeking his assurance that nothing so terrible could ever happen to them. He put his arm round her shoulders.

'Did either of you go out?'

'I did,' the husband answered. 'I made Pam stay because it was horrible enough inside, let alone out there hearing the noise, feeling the heat, and seeing David and Evelyn . . . I thought I might be able to do something. Of course, I couldn't do a bloody thing.'

'How long did you stay outside?'

He spoke to his wife. 'How long d'you reckon I was out?'

'It must have been about an hour.'

'I suppose you talked to people in the road?' asked Smith.

'Yes, of course.'

'Was there anyone there you didn't know?'

He looked puzzled.

'The reason for asking is that sometimes a fire is started by a person who's queer enough to get his kicks from watching it, so he stays around.'

'There wasn't anyone I didn't recognize except one man and he was talking to the Patricks who obviously knew him.' The husband hesitated, then said: 'Look, I'm terribly sorry, but I was due at the office half an hour ago. If there's any way I can help, any way at all, I'll stay on and ring and tell 'em I won't be in. But if there isn't, I ought to get moving.'

'No, I don't think there's anything more to ask you. Thanks for all your help.'

Out in the road, Smith looked back at the fire-damaged house. If he could get hold of the men who'd set this fire, he'd hang them with his own hands, without a second's thought or the slightest compunction.

.   .   .   .   .

In the brown-painted parade room at divisional H.Q., hung with photos of wanted men and snaps of local residents who were suspected of housebreaking, the duty sergeant said to the duty inspector: 'I've had a word with all the men on night turn and especially with the P.C. who had Hatton Close in his beat. None of 'em noticed any car which aroused suspicion and two three seven says that he checked the Close twice and neither time was there anything there.'

The duty inspector sighed. It had been a thin chance at best, but very occasionally thin chances turned up.

'Nothing in from Traffic?' asked the sergeant.

'Nothing useful.'

.   .   .   .   .

The nurse said: 'He got burned and quite badly bruised on his hip, but it's shock which is affecting him most. He's under sedation so you'll find him a bit confused.'

'I'll remember that,' said Campson.

'He's in the end bed, behind the screen. Keep the interview as short as you can and whatever you do, don't get him excited.'

Excited was a funny word to have used, thought Campson, as he walked down the ward: to him, excited suggested a pleasant course.

He parted the curtains and stepped inside. Roskill's head was bandaged, adding to the pallor of his face, and his eyes were underlaid by dark half moons of mental exhaustion.

Campson sat. 'My name's Detective Sergeant Campson. I'm terribly sorry about what's happened.' He paused. 'I'm afraid that now I've got to ask you some questions.'

Roskill nodded.

'Can you think of any reason why someone should have set fire to your house?'

He shook his head.

'You haven't recently had a row with anyone? I don't mean the kind you have with a neighbour when his dog keeps digging up your lawn, but the kind where people get really heated?'

'No.'

'Have you run into trouble with anyone at work?'

'No.'

'Could anyone think he's got a grudge against you because of money matters?'

'No.'

'Let's talk about the last few days. Have you seen any strangers around your house, or cars parked nearby, which you didn't recognize? Have there been any odd telephone calls with the line going dead as soon as the receiver's been picked up?'

'No.'

These were the answers which Campson had expected. If the fire had been set by the mob who were holding the town to ransom, then Roskill's house would have been chosen completely at random.

.   .   .   .   .

'How long have we got?' asked Menton, as he stood by the window of the room he was using. The strain under which he was working was making him look old and battered.

'All we can do is guess,' replied Fusil. 'There was a gap of one day between the first and second fire, but those two were to convince us they meant business.

There was a gap of two days between the second and this, the third one. You can see a sequence there and project it, but I don't think that's right. They've raised the ransom to four million. That's a hell of a sum, but one or two crimes around the world have just about matched it. The next step is eight million. Can they really expect to go for that much?'

'Why not?'

'It's difficult to explain precisely, but I reckon there's a point for most people at which large sums of money cease to be realistic. For me, eight million's no longer realistic.'

'Perhaps they're ambitious,' said Menton, with bitter sarcasm.

'All right, sir, that's hardly a definite point. So let's move on to the threats. We've had a small fire, a bigger one, and a fatal one. Now the pressure's really on, hard and biting. The public's seen photos of a stretcher with a sheet over it being carried out of a burned-out building and they know there was a twelve-year-old corpse under that sheet. They can clearly visualize their own families under sheets and they're really scared so they're going to demand, and go on demanding, that the ransom's paid and they can close down their imaginations. But if there's another fatal fire, even if several people get killed in it, that pressure is ironically going to slip just a fraction because it will all have happened before and so it becomes familiar and what's become familiar is part way to being accepted. Wars have proved that repeated horrors lessen their impact. So I reckon there'll be a pause now to let the maximum degree of public pressure break us.'

'In other words, you say we've got more time in which to track down these bastards?'

'That's right.'

'But you could be wrong. And if we play with time which we haven't got, there could be a fire with fifty, a hundred, people murdered in it.'

'There's always the possibility of being wrong.'

'But not with such terrible results.'

There was nothing more which could be said.

Menton brushed his hair back from his forehead with the palm of his hands. 'It's the helplessness that's choking me, Fusil. We don't know a damn thing more about this mob than when we started.'

'I know. I woke up in the middle of the night and went over and over the facts, trying to find out what we'd missed, what we weren't doing which we should. I couldn't think of a thing.'

'And you didn't get back to sleep either?'

.   .   .   .   .

The news was given out on the evening radio and TV broadcasts. Although the police had specifically asked that it be made clear that there was as yet still no absolute proof that the fatal fire had been the work of the blackmailing mob, the tragic incident was inevitably treated in a dramatic light and more than one commentator talked about the last warning before the threatened holocaust.

The phones in the operations room were inundated with calls: at one point fuses blew in the main telephone exchange. Before there had been disquiet, now there was something very close to panic. An innocent boy had been burned to death and the law had been unable to do anything to prevent this: if it could happen to one boy, it could happen to a hundred shoppers, or two hundred dancers in a discothèque, or three hundred listeners at a concert. People telephoned in to demand special protection, to name suspects, to describe in the minutest detail events which they now considered unusual. . . . The police simply couldn't keep up with the flood of information, despite the fact that many more men were drafted in to process and follow it up. And as the unchecked reports mounted in numbers, the detectives and uniform men vainly cursed because somewhere amongst those reports might lie the first lead they so desperately sought, yet by the time they came to it and recognized it for what it was they might easily be too late.

.   .   .   .   .

The mayor of Fortrow met the local M.P. in the latter's home. The mayor was the son of a Cypriot immigrant, a conservative, and the owner of a drapers which made a steady but unspectacular profit; the M.P. was labour, a very large landowner, and his house was a Georgian mansion which had been built for one of his ancestors. Since neither man had a marked sense of humour, they both failed to appreciate the irony of the circumstances.

The blue room at Veralem Hall, whose moulded ceiling had been designed by James Lunt the Younger, was the smaller of the two drawing-rooms. The furniture was early Georgian and very good, the five oil paintings were by a Victorian artist who had just come back into fashion, and in two large bow-fronted cabinets was the third best collection of seventeenth-century Japanese lacquer in the country. The enormous carpet was a rare Mortlake.

'What I want to know,' said the mayor, his voice roughly accented, 'is what are we going to do.'

'Quite so,' murmured the M.P., who often had difficulty in concealing his sardonic contempt for the ordinary man in whose name he helped to rule the country.

'It just ain't no good going on and on waiting for the police – they aren't getting anywhere.'

'I really don't think it's fair to speak quite like that when . . .'

'Fair or not, it's a fact. I've had a word with that detective in charge: very smooth and full of flam. But all what he said didn't add up to a damn thing. They've no idea who's behind the arson and they can't begin to guarantee there won't be a terrible tragedy.'

'We surely have to give them time?'

'Then has someone told them murdering bastards they've got to give 'em time as well?'

'Look, Alec, what I'm really saying is that at all costs we mustn't panic. After all, that's the whole object of the blackmailers: not to set another terrible fire, but to panic us into paying the ransom.'

'Their last letter said there ain't much time left.'

'The police have repeatedly advised against giving in to the demand.'

'What else d'you expect 'em to do? Admit straight off they can't do their job?'

'That's not being fair to them.'

'It's their job to protect us from murderers and it's clear they can't. So that money's got to be paid.'

'As a matter of fact, I did have a word with the Home Secretary over the phone on this point. Frankly, it's not going to be all that easy. Remember, it's not the country which is being held to ransom, it's Fortrow. So there is a case for saying that if the ransom has to be paid, Fortrow must find the money and as that obviously would take time . . .'

'He said that?'

'Précising his circumlocutory style, yes.'

'Then you get on back to that silly bastard and tell him to come and live in Fortrow for the next week and see if he still feels the same.'

The M.P. smiled. 'Rather too practical an exercise in politics for a man of his persuasion, I feel.'

15

Kerr walked away from the garage at which he had
been talking to one of the petrol-pump attendants. The
attendant had previously reported that a car owner had
stopped and bought four gallons of petrol in two two-
gallon cans. Wasn't that unusual at this time of the year
when no one was cutting grass or racing outboards? . . .
He'd agreed, thanked the man for being so observant,
and didn't point out that perhaps the car owner had a
chainsaw and made up his own two-stroke mixture or
a four-stroke cultivator and a lot of land to work. The
car number would be fed into the computer for identification, the owner questioned, and one more report
dealt with.

He came to a side road and stopped for the traffic and
as he waited he noticed the nameplate – Bretton Lane:
Mrs Prosser lived in this road. He hesitated, not wanting to 'waste' the time, but common sense assured him
that it would take much more time to make a special
journey here on some other occasion.

It took him over half an hour, during which time he
drank one gin and Mrs Prosser drank three and repeatedly informed him that he was the most handsome young
man she had ever met, to discover that she could tell
him nothing fresh about Albert Mickey's financial
circumstances: in so far as she had ever known, he'd
never had any money and where the fifty-two pounds
could have come from was a mystery.

Kerr went up to the room in which Mickey had lived and Mrs Prosser followed him, telling him in a husky voice that she hadn't the heart to clean out the place because the memories were still too painful. He suggested she return downstairs so as not to upset herself any further. For a while she was torn between the desire to see what was going on and to maintain the picture of a grief-stricken woman, then she finally left and went downstairs to the comfort of a fourth gin.

If Mickey *had* put the black on someone, then it must have been a strong black or Mickey would not have been murdered. In that case, he surely wouldn't have settled for a mere fifty-two pounds?

He hadn't shown any previous signs of wealth so it seemed likely he'd received the money only just before his death. What would he have done with the bulk of it? Put it in some kind of an account? But men of his stamp didn't normally go near banks or building societies, or other savings institutions, and amongst his effects there had been no cheque or pass book, or anything similar. He wouldn't have given it to anyone else to look after: his wife still hadn't been traced, but in any case they'd surely been parted far too long for him to let her into the secret? So he must have hidden the money. This room had been searched by the police, but the search had only been a routine one since there had been no reason at that time to suspect a large sum of money might be hidden.

There was one cupboard, smelling of stale dirt, with mouse droppings on the floor. Nothing in there. The gas ring was on a small metal shelf and the kettle contained only water. In the cupboard underneath were a few pieces of very cheap cutlery, plates, cups, and saucers, some rusting tins of food, a plastic bowl con-

taining something which had gone mouldy, a bottle
half filled with milk which had long since turned, and a
saucepan with a hole in the bottom. The floorboards
were worn, but firm throughout their length. The walls
were dirty and in need of painting, but unbroken. The
mattress felt as if it were filled with straw, but the cover
had no slit anywhere.

He lit a cigarette. Had Mickey hidden the money
somewhere else? Or were all assumptions wrong and had
he merely gone for fifty-two pounds plus a few he might
already have spent? Or was the whole story about his
blacking someone so much cod's?

He crossed to the door, opened it, and was just about
to step out into the corridor when he realized that he'd
committed the classical error of overlooking the obvious.

It took him less than a minute to discover that the
brass ball on top of the right-hand pillar of the bed
unscrewed. Inside the hollow pillar was wedged an
envelope thick with money.

    .   .   .   .   .

Fusil yawned. 'You haven't fingered any of the notes?'

Kerr, who stood by the side of the desk, said: 'No,
sir. Nor did I get my dabs on the flat of the envelope.'

'O.K. Tell Walsh to go over the envelope and every
single note inside.'

'That's not going to make him happy.'

'The only thing which does that is someone else's
catastrophe.'

    .   .   .   .   .

The door opened and Detective Sergeant Walsh
entered the room. He crossed to the desk and placed
two envelopes on this. From the first he brought out a

bundle of ten-pound notes. 'There's a hundred and twenty-five tenners there, sir. It's taken me hours to go over 'em and I've found God knows how many dabs and checked every last one of 'em out. They're all the same and they're all Mickey's.'

'It's not our lucky case, is it?'

Walsh's lugubrious expression suggested that no case was his lucky one.

Fusil picked up the bundle of money and flicked through it. 'Over a thousand quid: so it *was* a heavy blacking. What in the hell was it about? Who paid him that much, plus the money in his wallet, plus whatever he'd spent, to keep his mouth shut just long enough to organize his murder which was supposed to look like suicide and might have done if they'd got the knot right?'

'There's one more thing which might be of interest.'

'What's that?'

'The second envelope's the one the notes were found in. At the bottom of it are a few grains of powder.'

Fusil picked up the second envelope and ballooned it. He looked inside, then switched on the desk light and held the envelope directly under it. 'Any idea what it is?'

'None at all. I didn't notice the stuff until all the notes were out and then I decided I'd best leave it alone.'

He put the envelope up to his nose and smelled, but discerned no identifiable aroma. He licked the tip of his right forefinger. 'Hope to God it's not strychnine,' he said, before dipping his finger inside. He withdrew his finger and licked the tip a second time. 'Sugar – that's all.'

'So the division won't be needing a new D.I. after all,'

said Walsh, rather labouredly because jokes did not come easily to him.

Fusil stared down at the money. 'Who was he blacking? A small-time, unsuccessful crook who suddenly latched on to information so strong that he had to be croaked to keep him quiet. . . . Christ!' he suddenly exclaimed. 'I must be getting soft. Sugar!'

16

Kerr entered the bank and walked the length of the counter to the section marked 'Enquiries and Foreign Business'. He rang the bell and a woman, severe in looks, left the typewriter at which she'd been working and came across.

'Fortrow C.I.D. I'd like a word with the manager, please. It's very urgent.'

He had to wait only a couple of minutes before being shown into the manager's office. After a quick greeting, he said: 'I've two lots of bank notes here and we want to know what you can tell us about them.' Kerr put two envelopes on the desk.

'I suppose you know that these days we only keep a record of twenty-pound notes, simply because of the impossibility of being able to do more than that? So unless there are some twenties . . .?'

'I'm afraid there aren't.'

'Then I may not be able to help at all.' He emptied the first envelope and spread out the fifty-two pounds it had contained, separating the three ten-pound notes from the twenty-two one-pound ones. He carefully examined each note. 'No. Nothing on these. We won't have a record of their numbers, even if they were issued from this branch, and there aren't any distinguishing marks on any of them.' With precise movements, he collected up the notes and returned them to the envelope.

He emptied the second envelope. He riffled through the one hundred and twenty-five ten-pound notes. 'They're all pretty worn and dirty and about ready for parcelling up and sending back to be pulped. There doesn't seem to be any sequence of numbers.' He put the bundle down on the desk and then picked up each note in turn. When roughly half-way through, he examined one at very much greater length, finally putting it on one side. Before he had finished, he had placed two more notes with that first one.

He re-examined the three notes. 'Each one of these has had figures written on it – cashiers often write down how many notes are left in the bundle they keep in their float – so there's half a chance that someone will recognize her own writing. I'll go and find out.'

He returned to his office after ten minutes. 'It looks as if you're in luck after all. This ten-pound note . . .' He put it down on the edge of the desk. 'There are three sets of figures written on it in pencil and a seven appears in one of them and there's a bar through the upright in the Continental style. One of our cashiers was born and lived in France for a number of years and she's quite certain she wrote that set of figures because in addition to the bar there's a dot at the end and that's another invariable habit of hers. Have a look and you'll see what I mean.'

Kerr picked up the note. The bar to the upright was obvious, the dot at the end of the figures less so. 'Just how certain can she be?'

'I've told her to be ready to come and speak to you herself.' He used the internal telephone to ask her to come into his office.

She was – as Kerr immediately noticed – attractive in the traditional peaches-and-cream manner and clearly would never need to feel embarrassed when wearing a bikini.

'Miss Weaver, this is Detective Constable Kerr and he wants to question you about those notes I showed you just now.'

She turned to face Kerr.

He smiled at her in his warmest manner. 'What you've told the manager is going to be of tremendous help, so now there's just one more thing I've got to check up on – how certain are you that you wrote those figures? Don't get me wrong on this, Miss Weaver, I'm not doubting you in the slightest. But if you appeared in a court of law and were asked to say on oath that you did write those figures, would you be able to, or would you have to admit that although you're pretty certain, you can't be positive?'

She thought for a moment before answering: 'May I have another look?'

The manager handed her the note.

She studied the figures. 'I am quite positive I wrote those figures.'

'That's great. Thanks a lot for your help.'

After she had left, the manager picked up the note and stared at it. 'Miss Weaver issued this note so it probably circulated in this town. That means there's obviously a possibility it was paid back into this branch. In its present state, it would be condemned for pulping.' He looked up. 'The sack that was stolen in the raid here contained notes for pulping. Does that mean, then, that you may have discovered who carried out the raid?'

'The notes turned up in a case apparently totally unconnected with the bank raid. But it now looks as if there may be a connexion.'

'May you be able to say for sure whether there was

a traitor on the staff and to name him, or to clear everyone once and for all?'

'There has to be a chance of that now.'

The manager nodded. 'Good. I am quite certain everyone will be cleared.'

Kerr asked for another envelope and put the single pound note in this: on the outside he wrote the date, time, place, and the name of Miss Weaver, and finally he initialled it.

.   .   .   .   .

It was late evening and the north-east wind had increased to gale force: there were prolonged periods of heavy rain. Few people willingly went out and even the muggers, the drifters, and the slotters, stayed off the streets.

Fusil lit a cigarette which he'd taken from Campson because he'd run out of pipe tobacco. He was desperately tired, with his eyelids acting as if they'd weights attached to them, but he wouldn't take even a short break: he always had been a man who worked flat out.

Menton entered. He was looking ill: brain swirling tiredness had always affected him badly. 'I've just been speaking to the chief constable.' He slumped down on the edge of the desk. 'He's had the mayor and the local M.P. on the phone, and the Home Secretary's office, and for all I know Uncle Tom Cobbleigh as well. . . . Things are becoming critical.'

'It didn't need all them to point that out.'

'The pressure to pay the ransom is mounting all the time. If we will admit failure it'll be paid over to bring an end to the ransom demand – the only trouble then will be the arguments about who foots the bill.'

'We haven't failed.'

'I suppose strictly speaking we haven't until a second before the big fire breaks out. Then it's too late to admit that we have.'

'We've at last got a lead to work on.'

'A mighty thin one.'

'Thick enough.'

With dull curiosity, Menton stared at Fusil. Was it stubborn pride, a refusal to face the facts, or iron strength of mind which kept Fusil going? How fiercely did a man have to believe in himself not to be panicked by the thought that his actions might be sealing the fate of hundreds of people? 'Have you been on to the lab?'

'I have. And got my ears burned off for my pains. They'll let us know the moment they have any results, until then will we please leave them to work in peace.'

Menton slid off the desk and, shoulders slack, walked over to the window. He stared out at the wet night. Fusil stubbed out the half-smoked cigarette.

. . . . .

The phone rang, awakening Fusil who had fallen asleep in the chair. He jerked himself upright and tried to clear his mind of the fogs of sleep as he picked up the receiver.

'It's Forensic here. We've completed a full analysis of the powder – one hell of a job because there was so little of it. Powdered sugar and potassium chlorate.'

Fusil thanked the man, who sounded almost as tired as himself, and rang off. He picked up his pipe and opened the battered pouch before he remembered he'd no tobacco. He sucked on the empty pipe. Mickey had discovered the identity of one or more of the bank robbers and like the fool he was he'd jumped straight out of his class and had tried blackmail. The blackmailed man had paid him in order to keep him quiet long enough to arrange his murder. That money had been handled by someone who'd been in contact with the mixture probably used in the arson cases. Identify the bank robbers and probably one knew the identity of the arson mob. . . . The traitor in the bank could almost certainly name at least one of the bank robbers.

There'd never been enough time to concentrate sufficiently on the bank job. But what they had learned had surely pin-pointed the fact that if there were a traitor (he had no doubts), he had to be either Morgan or Hanna. Each had been investigated, each had been cleared.

There was an old police adage which was truer than most: 'When in doubt, go for the obvious.' Morgan claimed the money had been given to him by his wife's stepfather, Coutts. Coutts confirmed this and bank statements showed that he'd paid to Morgan a cheque for three thousand pounds. But . . . And Fusil suddenly saw that he'd missed something which should have been obvious, would have been if only he'd been able to give more time to the case.

He stood up, excitement jostling his thoughts together. He must interview Coutts and must have another member of the C.I.D. with him. That person should be Campson, but even in an emergency as severe as the present one Campson would always work according to the rules. When things got so tight they hurt, there was no room for rules, not if one worried more about results than the form in which these were achieved. He needed someone like himself, prepared when necessary to walk straight through the rule book. He rang through to the general room.

Kerr entered. His face was strained, his eyes bloodshot, his chin stubbled.

'Grab a seat,' said Fusil. 'The lab's just been on the blower. The powder in that envelope *was* sugar and potassium chlorate.'

Kerr whistled briefly. 'So there is a tie-up between the arson and the bank mobs.'

'I'd guess they're virtually the same. We know the bank job went sour on them and they only got away with a fraction of what they would have been hoping for – so they thought up this ransom job.' Fusil began to tap on the desk with his long fingers. 'We've got the lead we've been so desperately chasing.'

Kerr's voice was excited. 'Identify the traitor at the bank and make him name the man he sold the information to. . . . But we've worked on that line and got nowhere.'

'Which of the two suspects is the more likely?'

'Morgan, no question.'

'Where did that three thousand quid come from?'

'His wife's stepfather, Coutts. We traced it out.'

'All the way?'

'I don't get you, sir.'

'Did you ever check where *Coutts* got the three thousand from?'

Kerr slowly shook his head.

Fusil stood up. 'We've got to get the answers and get 'em bloody quick. That means putting on pressure. I want someone with me as a back-up, but as the pressure may have to be jammed on tight, I'm asking for someone to come with me, not ordering.'

Clearly, the D.I. was going to use whatever means

were necessary to force a confession, regardless of consequences. Because he had always tended to see his work as a crusade against evil, his career now meant little to him when the lives of innocent people were at stake. 'I'd like to go with you, sir,' said Kerr, knowing full well what the consequences of this decision could be.

17

By the time they arrived in Mayfield it was light and they could clearly see the farmhouse, mellowed by age until it was as much a part of the countryside as the huge ash to the right of it.

Fusil rang the front door bell. They waited, shivering in the wind, and soon they saw Coutts, dressed in pyjamas and a dressing gown, come down the stairs. He looked at them through the window by the side of the small porch and recognized Kerr. He unlocked the inner door and stepped into the porch, pulled open the outside door which was unlocked.

They went into the hall, cosily warm thanks to a large radiator. Fusil introduced himself and apologized for their early arrival but explained that the matter was very important.

Coutts, his expression reserved, said nothing but nodded and led the way into the sitting-room.

As Kerr, ducking under the lintel, followed Fusil inside, there were several sharp raps on the floor above.

'My wife will want to know who's visiting us this early in the morning,' said Coutts. 'Excuse me a moment while I go up and tell her.'

After he'd left the room, Kerr spoke in a low voice to Fusil. 'She's very ill and last time I was here she went on and on calling him upstairs.'

When Coutts returned, he stood in the centre of the room, just before the main beam which barely cleared the top of his head. 'I've told her who you are and re-assured her that I'm not about to be arrested and carted off to prison. Won't you sit down and tell me what this very urgent matter is all about?'

Very concisely, Fusil explained that there was now reason for believing there was a direct connexion between the bank robbers and the ransom mob and therefore it was vital to identify the former.

Coutts walked over to the window and stared out at the garden. 'I can follow that, of course, but why come here to tell me?'

'I remain convinced there was a traitor in the bank who gave that mob the information regarding the alarm system. If I can identify him, he'll be able to name to whom he sold the information.'

For a while Coutts didn't speak, then he swung round and his expression was now that of a man who was suffering. 'Do you swear you've told me the truth?'

'I promise you that the lives of a number of totally innocent people may well rest on what you tell me.'

There was more knocking on the floor above. Coutts looked up, his large, stubby-fingered fists clenched. 'I'll be up in a minute,' he shouted.

He returned to the centre of the room. 'She's dying,' he said abruptly. 'There's nothing can be done about it and it's been going on for months: often it feels more like years.' He jammed his fists into the pockets of his dressing-gown. 'The doctor won't listen to my pleas to be merciful and I haven't the guts to kill her myself. Does it shock you policemen to hear me talk about killing her?'

'No, sir, not at all,' replied Fusil. Kerr could not remember ever before hearing Fusil call any man 'sir' who was not his superior in the force.

149

'But if I can't help her physical self I can try to help her mental self by protecting her from other people's tragedies, especially her own family's. . . . She loves her daughter, Betty. I want to make that absolutely clear because if you've met Betty, you might wonder. And as Angela's illness has become worse, so her love for Betty has become more intense − I think that instead of resenting so much health and beauty, which she might have come to do because her own has gone, she gains strength from knowing that she'll leave behind what she once had. Perhaps you don't understand what I'm trying to say?'

'We understand perfectly,' said Fusil quietly.

Coutts went over to the chair to the right-hand side of the inglenook fireplace. 'Betty's happiness is Angela's happiness, Betty's unhappiness is her hell. So when Betty came here one day and told me . . .' He looked at Fusil. 'You must have guessed what happened, or you wouldn't have come here again?'

'I think so. Morgan gave you three thousand pounds to pay into your account so that you could then pay it to him. That meant there was a cheque, a credit entry in his account, and a debit entry in yours, to prove that you really had given him the money.'

'That's right. It was obviously something pretty shady so I told Betty I wouldn't do it. She immediately burst into tears and said Brian would be ruined, probably sent to jail, and what would all that do to her mother . . . I've often wondered how someone like Angela could have been so very unlucky. She's totally warm-hearted, totally honest, yet Betty is the most selfish person I've ever met. Betty knew exactly how to play the scene. If I wouldn't promise to help Brian, she couldn't control herself any longer and she'd have to pour out all her terrible troubles to her mother and that would upset her so terribly. . . .' Coutts's voice broke. He was silent for a while, then he continued in a firmer voice: 'I had to agree. Then when I learned what Brian must have done . . . I nearly told the truth. But the consequences of that were the same as before and in the end I didn't have the courage.'

'I think a very great many of us would have done exactly as you did, Mr Coutts.'

Coutts studied Fusil's face. 'You understand, don't you? A family can be hell because children can be so utterly ruthless. . . . What will happen now?'

'We'll return to Fortrow to question Brian Morgan.'

'I suppose everything that's happened will have to come out?'

'I'm afraid so.'

'So I merely succeeded in prolonging the agony.' He looked up briefly at the ceiling. 'Unless that other agony comes to an end very soon.'

Fusil and Kerr said very brief good-byes and they had driven over a mile before Fusil spoke and then it was on a matter unconnected with what had just taken place.

They reached Morgan's house at eight-fifteen. Fusil said: 'Didn't you once describe the wife as looking like Helen of Troy and Cleopatra rolled into one?'

'Something along those lines,' replied Kerr.

'How would you go about describing the husband?'

'Ordinary and pretty weak natured – only I can't quote any particular reason other than general impressions for saying that.'

'It figures. Let's go and find out how weak.'

Betty Morgan opened the front door. She was dressed in tight-fitting sweater and slacks which made it unnecessary to wonder if she had all the right curves.

In answer to Fusil's query, she said: 'But Brian's about to go off to work. Can't you come back some other time?'

'I'm afraid not.'

She looked at him with a little girl/big girl expression on her face. 'Are you just going to ask him all the old questions?'

'Not this time. We've some new ones for him.'

'Oh!' she hesitated. 'I suppose you'd better come along into the sitting-room, then, and I'll call him.' She left, body swaying provocatively.

Brian Morgan entered in less than a minute. He was wearing a dark, pin-striped suit, well worn yet still reasonably smart. 'Betty said you wanted a word. Anything I can do, I'll be only too glad to help.' His manner was earnest. 'By the by, I'm sure you'd like the heater on – it gets a bit parky these mornings, doesn't it?'

They didn't answer and Morgan began to talk too quickly about the poor weather. He carried a fan heater over from the far side of the room and plugged this in and switched it on. 'Would you care for coffee? Betty can easily make some.'

'There's no need to bother,' said Fusil quietly. 'D'you mind if I smoke a pipe?' He packed his pipe with some tobacco he'd borrowed from a sergeant. 'Have you got your notebook ready?' he asked Kerr. He struck a match and lit the pipe. Then he looked up and spoke to Morgan. 'Why not sit down? We're liable to be here quite a time.'

'But I can't hang on here. . . .' Faced by their bland indifference to what he said, he became silent. Slowly, irresolutely, he went over to the settee and sat. He fiddled with a strand of hair which hung down over his forehead.

Fusil said: 'We know you accepted a bribe of three thousand for passing on the details of the alarm system at the bank. What we want to hear now is who paid you and who you gave the details to.'

'I didn't do anything of the sort,' he blustered. 'I told him . . .' He pointed at Kerr. 'I wouldn't ever do anything like that. . . .'

'You tried to get Mr Coutts to help you voluntarily and when he refused you forced him into doing it. He's told us how you viciously blackmailed him,' added Fusil contemptuously. 'You gave him the three thousand so that he could then pay you the money and the records would appear to show that everything was above board.'

Morgan's face twisted with fear.

'Who gave you the three thousand?'

'No . . . no one.'

'Can't you understand you're at the end of the road? There are no desperately ill women or their frantic husbands left for you to blackmail emotionally to help get you out of trouble.'

The carriage clock on the mantelpiece struck the half hour. Morgan said shrilly: 'I've got to go to work. I can't stop any longer. You'll have to come back some other time. . . .'

Fusil just shook his head.

'Oh God!' whispered Morgan.

Kerr spoke in friendly tones. 'Tell us what happened and get it over and done with. There's no point in going on and on denying everything when we know what happened. Right now, the more you lie, the worse you make things for yourself.'

Morgan looked entreatingly at Kerr, as if he thought that perhaps the detective would absolve him from everything.

'It was your wife who persuaded you, wasn't it?'

Morgan shook his head, but his mouth was working. Then he suddenly spoke wildly. 'Betty wanted things: things I couldn't afford. She wouldn't stop telling me that all our friends kept having new clothes, cars, furniture, but that I wouldn't buy her anything. . . . At night, she wouldn't . . . She'd smile and say she'd a headache, but she knew I knew she was lying. And she went out of her way to make things more difficult for me. You can't imagine what it was like. She used to walk around with nothing on and say . . . And say how much she wanted me. But then when I . . . She'd start on again about all the things we needed and if I wouldn't buy them for her, why should she do anything nice for me . . . I was going crazy.'

'When was the first approach made to you to pass on the details of the bank alarms?' asked Fusil.

'There was a phone call.' Morgan stared miserably into space. 'Three thousand for the information and no one would ever know a thing. I told the man to go to hell. But Betty wanted to know what it was all about. And d'you know what?' He sounded pitifully surprised. 'She couldn't understand why I'd refused. She said that with three thousand she could have some of the things she needed and go to some of the places she wanted to go to.

'I tried to tell her, I was in a position of trust. She didn't seem to be able to understand. She just sneered at me for being soft and when we went to bed that night . . . She swore she wouldn't know me that way again because I wouldn't do anything for her. I tried not to want her so much, I swear I did, but it was hopeless.

'I knew there might be a police investigation, so I thought up the idea of paying the money into Henry's account. Of course, at first he wouldn't hear of the idea. He's always been so completely . . . honest. Then Betty managed to persuade him to agree.'

'Who gave you the three thousand? To whom did you give the plans?'

Morgan shook his head.

'Don't be bloody silly.'

'I can't. I won't.'

'The men who used you are mixed up in the ransom and arson that's going on now, here in Fortrow. They've murdered twice already. They're threatening to murder God knows how many more people.'

'I'm not going to tell you anything more.'

Fusil put down his pipe and spoke to Kerr. 'Forget the notebook.' He watched Kerr shut his notebook. He spoke quite slowly. 'I saw the kid who was burned to death in Hatton Close when they pulled his body out of the house and I talked to his parents. Ever seen a human body that's been burned? Ever spoken to parents mad with grief? If I don't get the names there could be dozens more bodies and dozens and dozens more husbands and wives, parents, or children, all mad with grief.

'Forget your own miserable little self for once. Try to make up for a fraction of the harm you've done. Who gave you the money? Who did you give the plan to?'

'I can't tell you.'

Fusil stood up. 'I don't like violence. I spend my life fighting it. But just once in a while there's a time when

155

it's necessary because nothing else will work. You're either going to give names or I'm going to smash them out of you.'

'No!'

Fusil stepped forward, knowing that he was throwing away his career, but certain that this coward could be forced to talk.

Kerr said: 'Just a moment, sir.'

'Keep out of this,' Fusil retorted fiercely.

'No, sir.' Kerr spoke to Morgan. 'When I visited Mr Coutts's house I saw a photo in the sitting-room. It was probably taken just after the marriage between him and Mrs Coutts when your wife was still a girl.'

Morgan was trembling.

'With her was a boy, a little bit older. He must have been her brother. What's happened to him? Why doesn't anyone ever mention him? Why was Mr Coutts even more bitter over his wife's family than the apparent circumstances seemed to warrant. Why is Mrs Coutts so desperate to believe in your wife's happiness that you and your wife could blackmail Mr Coutts into helping you over a crime? Is it because her son had turned rotten a long time ago and now she's only her daughter left to believe in and so to be forced to learn her daughter was as rotten as her son would leave her to die in total despair?'

Morgan shut his eyes.

'It was her brother who bribed you?' said Fusil, making it as much a statement of fact as a question.

Morgan nodded.

'What name's he using?'

'Joe Allsopp,' mumbled Morgan.

'Where's he living?'

'I don't know.'

'Goddamn it . . .'

'I swear I don't know: no one in the family does. Every time he just suddenly turns up or telephones.'

Fusil was certain he was telling the truth. He put his pipe in his pocket, jerked his head at Kerr, and walked over to the door.

They were crossing the hall when Betty came out of the kitchen. 'I do hope everything's all right now? Won't you stay and have some coffee or tea?' she asked. Fusil stared at her with such contempt that she drew in her breath and stepped back.

18

Fusil said over the telephone: 'Joe Allsopp. I want every single known detail about him with particular reference to all recorded contacts and addresses. Maximum priority.' He replaced the receiver, leaned back in the chair, and stared at Kerr, who was perched on the edge of the desk. 'You saved me from doing something drastic back in Morgan's house. Thanks a lot.'

They waited. Miss Wagner came into the room and began to tell Fusil that he had forgotten to do something important, but he stopped her so brusquely that for once she did not press the point but left, very straight-backed.

The phone rang. Fusil crossed to the desk and answered it. He listened, then said he wanted the file right away. He spoke to Kerr after ringing off. 'Nothing until he was nineteen but since then he's made up for lost time. Last known job was a big payroll snatch. He uses violence and is considered a very smart operator to work for.'

'What's his last known address?'

'In south Clapham.'

'Why hasn't he been questioned as a potential suspect?'

'For all we know at this moment he has been, but there can't have been any hint that he was tied up with the ransom. If, in fact, he is.'

'D'you think, then, that despite everything maybe he isn't?'

Fusil shook his head. 'When things start fitting at this stage of a case, they're usually right.' He telephoned London and asked for Allsopp's last address to be visited and full enquiries to be made to try and trace his present whereabouts.

.   .   .   .   .   .

The chief constable sat behind his ornate desk and the assistant chief constable, shoulders hunched to make him look even more like a battered ex-pug, stood by the window.

'Fusil's calling for more time,' said the chief constable. 'Doesn't the man realize the pressures we're under?'

'Probably not. That's the advantage of being in the field.' He turned. 'On second thoughts, though, remembering the man, he probably doesn't give a damn.'

'How far has he got?'

'They're hoping to close in on Allsopp and through him identify the rest of the mob. But how long it'll take to locate Allsopp . . .' The assistant chief constable shrugged his shoulders.

'With the record he's got, Allsopp's not going to start talking the moment they take him in, any more than any others in the mob will.'

'Obviously not.'

'So if he keeps his mouth tight shut, will Fusil have enough on him to hold him?'

'Not unless he finds some solid proof at the time of the pick-up.'

'Then clearly he may have to let him go. Which means the mob will know how close we've got. In the same way, even if Fusil can hold him but doesn't learn enough to make a clean sweep, his detention will tell the mob just as loudly and clearly. In either case they'll know they've got to move and move very quickly, so the crisis will be precipitated which everyone now is working like hell to avoid. We're on a hiding to nothing.'

'So do we call Fusil off?'

'We'd be bloody poor policemen if we did that. But we have to accept that when he goes in it will probably be the end for us.'

.   .   .   .   .

The detective sergeant with his pointed face and quick, sinuous movements, had something of the look of a ferret. He spoke over the phone to one of his informers. 'I'm looking for Joe Allsopp. He's supposed to live in your territory.'

'Joe Allsopp?' said the informer, as if the name were new to him. His voice was hoarse. He'd once had his throat cut, but the knife hadn't gone quite deeply enough to complete the job.

'It'll pay heavy.'

'I ain't seen him around recent, mister.'

'Maybe you've heard which way he travelled?'

'Could've been south.'

'To where?'

'I wouldn't know and that's straight. Joe don't talk much.'

'Who does he move around with when he's in the Smoke?'

'I've seen him with Angel, but no one else. Bit of a loner is Joe.'

'Is that Angel Race?'

'S'right, mister.'

'Is he still around?'

'I ain't seen him for a bit, neither.'

.   .   .   .   .

It was nearly midday by the time photographs of Joe Allsopp and Angel Race had been copied and the copies had been distributed around the division. It was one-forty-five when P.C. Cleveland, along with a number of other P.C.s about to start late turn, entered the Parade Room at divisional H.Q.

The duty sergeant called out: 'All of you, take a butchers at the board.' He pointed to one of the notice boards which had been cleared so that two photographs could be prominently displayed.

The P.C.s studied the photos.

'Have any of you clapped eyes on either of those beauties in the past few days or weeks?'

'I reckon I have, Sarge,' said P.C. Cleveland.

'Which one?'

'Angel Race.'

'When and where?'

The P.C. took his notebook from his coat pocket and methodically thumbed through it. He read an entry. 'Five nights ago, Sarge. I got called to the Fox and Geese because a couple of tearaways had tanked up too much and were causing a disturbance. I sorted them out just in time for one of the cars to turn up to give a hand.' There was some laughter. (Question: How d'you know if a bloke's ever worked on the cars? Answer: He never arrives until all the trouble's over.) 'I asked two or three blokes for their names and addresses as witnesses and this bloke in the photo was one of 'em. As I remember it, he wasn't over keen to speak up.'

'What name did he give?'

He read out three names: none of them was Race.

   .   .   .   .   .

Every known criminal, informer, and prostitute, who lived within a mile of the Fox and Geese was questioned in one of the fastest operations the division had mounted for a long time.

'Who d'you say he was?' asked Eddie Paradine, who stood less than five feet tall, but whose shoulders were broad enough for a six-footer.

'I didn't give a name,' replied the sergeant. 'Have a look at this.' He handed over a photo.

Paradine studied it briefly. 'Never clapped eyes on the bloke.'

'Come off it. He's been seen in your territory. If a kid nicks a handful of sweets in your territory you know all about it.'

'Sarge, straight as a ruler, I ain't never clapped eyes on the bloke.' He handed the photo back.

'I don't believe you, Eddie?'

'Now would I ever lie to you?'

'And because I don't believe you, I'm going to keep on asking you questions and when I get tired I'll send a couple of blokes along to take my place. Could get bad for business, I suppose.'

You suppose! thought Paradine, and his face screwed up with an expression of bitter, impotent hatred. Let a man steer a course only a fraction outside the law and the splits shoved in their boots with callous viciousness.

'Well?' said the sergeant.

'He's living down Escotts Road.'

'On his own?'

'With a bird.'

'Thanks a lot, Eddie: been a great help.'

Bastards, he silently shouted.

* * * * *

Menton, sitting behind Fusil's desk, looked up, his heavy face showing a most unusual indecision. 'It's a complete gamble.'

'I know,' replied, Fusil. 'So maybe we could offer Race some sort of a deal ... .'

'No deals,' snapped Menton immediately.

'Look sir, we just can't afford to keep an eye on every dot and comma in the rule book . . .'

'You'll stick to the rules, whatever the pressures, whatever the crisis. D'you understand that?'

Fusil had been a fool to say what he had. He knew Menton genuinely believed that if a man went outside the rules he was betraying the law he was supposed to be serving. Perhaps his attitude called for respect: Fusil could not respect it.

'And what chance is there of finding a lead through to the rest of the mob?' asked Menton, as if there had been no short, sharp clash between two men who saw the world differently. 'Race is a real pro. D'you think anyone from the mob will have visited the house for other people to see? All contacts will have been made well away from there. And as no grasser's come through with any hard news, all their meetings have been blacked out.'

'Don't forget there's the woman.'

'He'll have kept her completely in the dark.'

'Then do we sit back and shout Kamerad and do nothing about following up the lead?'

It was the same question, if concerning a different man, that the chief constable had discussed. Menton had to give the same kind of an answer. 'You follow it up and you do every goddamn thing possible to break the case. But when you move you're starting a time clock that hasn't got very long to run. So if you fail, you accept that failure.' He slumped back in his chair. 'Remember that, Bob,' he said, must unusually using Fusil's Christian name. 'You accept that failure. You can't win 'em all.'

'I can try.'

Menton sighed. And you couldn't make a leopard change its spots.

19

The house was almost at the end of Escotts Road, opposite a factory which had been shut down two years before and was still empty with gappy, broken windows. It was an ordinary, graceless, semi-detached: there was a tiny front garden and a larger back garden, part of which had a garage on it. This garage fronted a dirt road which separated the gardens of Escotts Road from those of Ponders Avenue.

The police, all in civvies, arrived after dark in two small separate parties in order to attract as little attention as possible. Fusil, a W.P.C., and a P.C., arrived first, Kerr, a sergeant, and a P.C., five minutes later.

Race was a large man, who took considerable pride in keeping fit. He had a square, not unhandsome face, full of hard character. On his right cheek were several small scars which had been caused by three safety razor blades set in a raw potato: surgeons had done wonders, but they hadn't been able to hide all the damage. Connie Smith was younger than Race, snappily attractive, scared but trying very hard not to show it.

'Take her through to another room, Joan,' Fusil said to the W.P.C.

'I'll get my lawyer to . . .' shouted Connie, as she left. The door of the sitting-room shut to cut off her threat.

Race had sprawled out on the settee, his long legs stuck straight out. He looked bored.

Fusil nodded and the two P.C.s and the sergeant left the room, making a point of firmly shutting the door behind them.

'Have a smoke?' asked Fusil.

'Sure,' said Race. He helped himself to one of his own cigarettes.

'Give the man a light,' said Fusil to Kerr.

Race flicked open a gold lighter before Kerr had drawn his throw-away gas lighter out of his coat pocket.

Fusil sat down in one of the armchairs and there was a twanging of springs. 'That needs something done to it,' observed Race. 'I'll get the repairers in tomorrow.'

Fusil said pleasantly: 'You and Joe Allsopp are part of the mob who did the bank job in the summer. That blew up in your faces because you didn't know the sacks of notes were stacked on a weight alarm. Because you didn't get the loot you were expecting, you decided to make your fortunes in another way – you'd hit this town for a few million quid in ransom. So far you've torched a Dutch barn, a garage, and a house in which a kid of twelve was burned to death.'

'That's getting personal, Inspector. I've had my moments, no arguing, but burning houses with kids in em? Do you mind?'

'Interested to know how we traced you?'

'Be my guest.'

'When Albert Mickey tried to put the black on you, you paid him off with some of the few notes you did manage to nick from the bank. Carelessness.'

'We can't all get triple As.'

'They were identified by a cashier. That told us the attempted ransom was tied up with the abortive bank raid. So we went back to the bank job and finally identified Brian Morgan as the link-man.'

'I know a Butch Morgan. After a couple of pints of Liffey water he'll whistle "The Bonnie Banks o' Loch Lomond" like you've never heard it whistled before.'

'Morgan identified Joe Allsopp.'

'I've met a bloke called Alton who could whistle "What shall we do with the drunken sailor" whilst drinking a pint of whisky.'

'You and Joe have worked together on these fires. The last one, which killed a kid of twelve, has turned it into a murder rap.'

Race looked down at his hands to inspect his nails.

'The judge will be wondering whether to make it thirty or forty years minimum even before he starts the trial. So the blokes who actually did the torching aren't going to watch their grandchildren grow up. But I don't suppose it will go so hard on the ones who stayed at home that night because the law's got soft and doesn't handle constructive murder as it used to. . . . You know something? If it were me, I'd make sure people understood I wasn't near that house when it was torched.'

'So where were you?' asked Race. He flicked his cigarette into the fireplace.

'Who did the actual torching?'

'Now why ask me?'

Fusil stood up and the springs twanged again.

'Musical chairs,' said Race.

'Get up and strip.'

Race said sweetly: 'I didn't know you were one of them.'

'You saw the three blokes who are waiting outside. They're dead eager to get their hands on one of the blokes who torched a twelve-year-old kid.'

Race slowly stood up. 'I've a mind to write to *The Times* to complain.'

'Remember my name's spelt with an I not an E.'

.   .   .   .   .

They'd searched him and his clothes: they'd searched the house, room by room: they'd found nothing.

'Send someone down to cover the garage and the car,' said Fusil, not bothering to hide his bitter disappointment.

The sergeant left the bedroom in which their search had finished. 'How do we play it now, sir?' asked Kerr.

'Go back and try the woman a second time,' he answered wearily.

'But she doesn't seem to know anything . . .'

'She doesn't. But it's something to do to help keep us from thinking.'

They went down to the sitting-room.

'You've no right to keep me here,' complained Connie, in a high, whining voice.

Fusil ignored her and spoke to the W.P.C. 'Have you tried to explain the situation to her again?'

The W.P.C. nodded her tightly curled head. 'I've said how anyone who had anything at all to do with the job is responsible in law. I've told her that the people who actually set the fire will probably spend the next thirty or forty years in the nick . . .'

'I don't know anything,' shouted Connie wildly. 'Just because I'm here with Angel, that don't signify. How many more times have I got to say that?'

'Which of his friends has he been seeing?' demanded Fusil.

'No one's ever come here. All the time it's been just him and me and when he's been in a temper, that's been one too many.'

'Who did you meet when you went out together?'

'No one. Do I have to tell you in letters ten feet high? There's never been anyone at all.'

'It would make things a lot smoother for you if you decided to help us.'

'Oh God!' she said, apparently addressing the Picasso print of a triangularly dislocated woman on the opposite wall. 'You tell 'em again and again and still they won't listen. So how d'you get through to them?'

'Give us a name and you'll have a hot line.'

'Father Christmas.' She swung round. 'I've been with him for five months. Right? And when he's not drunk or bloody minded, he's fun: him and me have had some good laughs together. But in all that time he's never told me anything and I've never met any of his friends and when he's gone off on his own he's never said where he's been. Shall I say it all again. In all the time . . .'

'All right, we get the message,' said Fusil.

'So?'

'So now I believe you.'

'Then I'm clearing out of here fast.'

'You're not moving.'

'But why?' she cried, in frightened despair.

Why? He didn't know. He said to the W.P.C., 'Keep her happy,' then led the way out to the hall.

He walked over to the small table window, opposite the foot of the stairs, and stared out at the tiny front garden, a mass of weeds and an overgrown privet hedge. Menton had warned him, but in his heart he'd hoped. The search would turn up something vital. Race would decide to betray the others in an effort to save himself. The woman would let drop some vital fact . . . But they'd uncovered nothing, learned nothing.

Before, they'd at least had time. Now, they had none.

He hadn't anything on Race, so he must let him go. Within hours, the mob would know the danger and they'd react immediately and viciously, giving the town a deadline, making every householder look with terror at his family. . . . The four million would have to be paid. The police would try to be in on the hand-over, but this mob would know what arrangements to make to ensure that the police had only an outside chance. . . .

He jammed his hands into his pockets. Menton had said that he couldn't win them all and he'd replied that he could try. He'd tried and failed.

The sergeant returned through the kitchen to the hall. 'We've been through the garage and the car, sir. There's nothing except these which were under the front passenger seat. I'm afraid they're only old car-park tickets.' He handed them over.

Because the flimsy paper had originally been scrumpled up, it was difficult to read the faint blue printing, but he could just make out that both tickets had been issued for Fortrow Municipal Council, both cost twenty pence, one was timed nineteen hundred and ten hours and the other nineteen hundred and fourteen hours. He was about to discard them as completely valueless, as had the sergeant, when he noticed that the two date's now over a month back, were exactly a week apart. He thought for a moment, then walked across to the door into the sitting-room and went inside. The P.C. was sitting upright in the armchair which didn't twang and Race was still sprawled out on the settee, watching the TV.

Race said: 'You're beginning to remind me of that play about a man who came for dinner, but stopped on for weeks.'

'I've been talking to Connie.'

'Just so long as things didn't get complicated. Her fortune's not in her brains.'

'I asked her if you and she went out a lot together.'

'You should have got her to show you our social diary.'

'She said you often went out on your own.'

'A bloke sometimes needs to be on his tod.'

'So his girl doesn't see who he's meeting?'

Race realized his previous answer had been an unwise one. 'That's right. Try to chat up another bird when she's around and there's war.'

'Or chat up Joe Allsopp and there's a witness.' Fusil brought out the tickets from his pocket. 'These were under the front passenger seat of your car: car park tickets for the same time two Thursday evenings, a week apart. I suppose that's when you were meeting Allsopp and preparing the job?'

Race laughed. But just for a second there had been a look of consternation in his eyes.

20

Fusil paced the hall, keeping to the carpet to deaden his footsteps. Kerr, using the soft technique, was trying to lull Race into admitting something. Fusil suffered an urge to go into the sitting-room to discover whether he were succeeding, but knew that it would be ridiculous to do so. From the dining-room came the sound of Connie's voice, loud and whining, followed by the W.P.C.'s quieter, deeper-pitched one.

Race's consternation had been short, but sharp. Merely reaction to the guilty knowledge that he had met Allsopp at least twice in the car park while they planned the ransom job? Or reaction to something far more dangerous? He spoke to the sergeant who sat on the stairs.

'Get these two tickets to someone from the town hall who can identify from the serial numbers which car park it was. You'll have to chase the bloke up in his home so when he starts moaning tell him it's a matter of life and death. Possibly his.'

'That's about the only thing which will get anyone from the town hall moving after hours,' said the sergeant, as he stood up and came down the stairs.

'Ring me here, so get the number before you go.'

The sergeant went over to the telephone which stood on a small corner cupboard and wrote down the number on the back of an envelope.

Fusil resumed his pacing of the hall. This was their final chance. If it were a chance.

.   .   .   .   .   .

The telephone rang and Fusil lifted the receiver but said nothing, in case the call was for Race or Connie.

'Sergeant Tomburn here, sir.'

'Let's have the news.'

'The car park's an unmanned one with an automatic barrier in Astrid Road, which is at the back of Eckbourne Road: left at the traffic lights if you're heading south.'

He swore.

'What was that, sir?'

'Frustration. . . . Get out to the car park now and I'll meet you there.' He replaced the receiver. He'd been hoping again, hoping that Race had parked in that car park because it was close to the building they had chosen for their target if the ransom wasn't paid and they had to torch somewhere occupied by a number of people. But Eckbourne Road was a shopping centre and along it were also a couple of restaurants, several snack bars, a cinema . . . Dozens of fat targets. Impossible to pick out the most likely one.

He left the house and drove with more than his usual selfishness through the back streets to Eckbourne Road. It was dark, cold, and dampening, an evening to be sitting in front of a roaring fire watching the telly, but even so a large number of people were along the road, eating, drinking, watching films.

The lights were set at red, but nothing was coming out of Astrid Road so he shot them and turned left: a woman, walking a small dog, waved her arm at him to express her annoyance at his road manners.

He stopped by the entrance to the car park, which was on the right, and stepped out on to the pavement. The sergeant, who'd been fifty yards further along, came up but said nothing. Fusil looked to his right and left. Apart from a modern, institutional looking building with wide glass windows, all the houses in the road were large, probably late Victorian or Edwardian, probably converted into flats or offices. He swore. Still more prime targets. 'D'you know what that place is?' he finally asked, pointing to the institutional building on the other side of the road, thirty yards to their left.

'It's the local public library, sir.'

'Which, no doubt, shuts dead on time so it won't be open after seven at night.'

'The only thing is, I believe this one's got a lecture hall. So it could be open later on.'

'We'll go over and see.'

They crossed the road and walked along the pavement. There was a small car park to the side of the library and in front of this was a sculpture in some earth-coloured stone, three feet high, which looked as if a child of four had been having fun with plasticine.

'I'll bet that load of cod's put a few pence on the rates,' said the sergeant morosely. 'The sculptor's probably the mayor's nephew.'

There were four stone steps leading up to the double front door of toughened glass, which was recessed so that it stood under the cover of the top floor. Looking through the door they could see a noticeboard on an easel and there was sufficient light from outside for them to read the notices. There was a list of lectures for the month and amongst them was: 'Every Thursday at seven-thirty. Road safety and Better Driving. Lecturer, a member of the county constabulary.'

Fusil remembered the sick humour of the ransom notes and he knew with a violent, exciting certainty that to such men nothing would be funnier than torching a building in which the police were giving a lecture on road safety to the public.

.   .   .   .   .

He parked outside Race's house, but did not immediately get out. How to avoid the inevitable? If they took Race in for questioning, he'd outlast them. Probably before that his disappearance would alarm the mob. In either case they must, inevitably, change the target.

Did the four million they were demanding really count when placed against the lives of an unknown number of innocent people? How far was his own pride involved. . . . He hoped not at all, but surely no man could ever be certain what motives truly moved him? Shouldn't he report to Menton and admit defeat?

An oncoming vehicle on dipped headlights passed, momentarily illuminating the interior of his car. His attention was caught by something white, seen from the corners of his eyes, and he turned to look at the back shelf. It was a newspaper, thrown there three days before and then forgotten even though it contained an article he'd particularly wanted to read.

A newspaper! he suddenly thought.

Menton would be furious – and afraid. But once things were moving no one would be able to stop them, not if the mob reacted as he was certain they would, provided only that the fire lit under their tails was hot enough. . . .

He climbed out of the car, crossed to the front door of the house, and rang the bell. A P.C. let him in. He went straight into the dining-room.

'For God's sake,' shouted Connie, 'what's going on? I've been stuck in . . .'

'Shut up and listen hard,' he said.

She looked nervously at him, then moved her chair fractionally closer to the W.P.C.

He sat and brought tobacco pouch and pipe from his pocket and slowly filled the pipe, repeatedly tamping the tobacco with his forefinger.

'Well, ain't you ever going to say anything?' she demanded, her voice very shrill.

'We've nailed 'em,' he said. He saw the surprised look on the W.P.C.'s face. 'For bank robbery, arson, and murder. And d'you know what finally helped us to nail 'em? Something you told me.'

'Me? But I ain't . . .'

'I told Angel you'd helped us. Made him shout.' He shook his head. 'Never thought it'd take him like that.'

'Jesus!' she whispered, in anguished prayer.

'We've no cause to hold you any longer, so you're free to go.' He looked up. 'Know what I'd do if I were you, Connie?' She stared at him, quite terrified. 'I'd get on the first main line train out of Fortrow Central and I'd keep travelling until I reached the last stop and then I'd hide until it's all over and they're safely inside for the next thirty years.'

After a while, she said: 'I never told you nothing, you know that.' She began to cry.

Fusil spoke to the W.P.C. 'See her on to a train.'

'Yes, sir,' said the W.P.C., not understanding what was happening, not quite managing to hide her contempt for what Fusil had done.

He didn't watch them leave, but stared into space. After a while, he realized his pipe had gone out and he relit it. Fernley Green would do, he finally decided: a country town, small, where the magistrates were old school and went out of their way to support the police. They'd hold Race there for as long as they dared and then they'd bring him up before the magistrates and ask for a week's remand in custody, quoting evidence which couldn't be successfully challenged immediately. . . .

. . . . .

Fusil parked in front of Harvey's house. He walked along the crazy-paving path to the front door and rang the bell. A woman's voice called out: 'Who is it?'

'Mary, it's Bob. Bob Fusil.'

He heard a bolt being withdrawn and then the door opened and light spilled over him. 'Sorry to keep you waiting, Bob, but these days we don't open the door at night until we know who's the other side.' Mrs Harvey was plump and one of the warmest characters he knew.

'I'm sorry to butt in this late, but it is very urgent. Is Fred in?'

'He's watching the telly fast asleep, as always! I keep saying, why not go to bed, but you know Fred, grandfather to a mule.'

Harvey woke up as they entered the over-warm sitting-room and, blinking blearily, wriggled into an upright position.

'It's Bob,' his wife said loudly.

'I can see that: so now I'm wondering what in the hell he wants.'

'I'm after a favour,' said Fusil.

'Not a chance in hell.'

'Sit down, Bob,' said Mrs Harvey, 'and I'll go into the kitchen and make a pot of tea.' She saw that he was about to refuse. 'It'll be no trouble. I always have a cup

177

last thing. It helps me to sleep through his snoring.' She left.

Fusil sat. He said: 'First off, I'll give you the story so far, right off the record.' Briefly, he told Harvey what had happened.

'Goddamn it, Bob,' snapped Harvey, 'why come here in the middle of the night and wake me up from a wonderful dream which included two blondes if it's only to tell me something I can't print?'

'I had to explain why you're going to do me a favour. Has the paper been put to bed yet?'

Harvey looked at the carriage clock on the mantel-piece. 'If the night editor hasn't died, it's just about there now.'

'Then phone him up and tell him to hold things because there's a last-minute change. You've a report from a police spokesman which says quite categorically that there will be no dealings whatsoever with the ransom mob, no matter what threats are made. You've learned that this hard attitude is because considerable progress in the investigations has been made. According to a reliable source, vital information has been received from an informer which will lead to the identification of the men behind the ransom threat. The police have refused to confirm or deny this.

'You also want a photo printed of a crashed Ford Granada whose number plate doesn't show and a short paragraph saying the car was involved in a crash early on tonight. The two occupants suffered very serious injuries and the driver, Adam Race, was found to be dead on arrival in hospital. His companion, Miss Connie Smith, is in an intensive care unit.'

Harvey swore with bemused admiration.

21

A chair creaked. 'Can't you sit still?' Fusil whispered angrily.

'Sorry, sir,' said one of the P.C.s. Almost immediately that chair, or another, creaked yet again.

None of them could keep still, thought Fusil: movement somehow helped to lessen the tension. And it was worse for the others in the children's section of the library because they could see nothing except, very dimly, the rows of books on the walls. Probably they were imagining the torchers slipping through unnoticed, a blast of explosion and fire, and themselves trapped, surrounded by Robert Louis Stevenson, A. A. Milne, and Enid Blyton.

He recalled Menton's disbelief and fury of three days ago. 'You've what? Have you gone crazy? Don't you bloody understand . . .' And then he'd stopped because it was so obvious that Fusil didn't understand. When he'd spoken again he'd regained some self-control and in cutting terms he'd made it perfectly clear that if things didn't work out he'd personally see that Fusil suffered the full consequences of his own stupidity.

By the grace of God, lies, and magistrates who would prefer to believe a uniform inspector rather than St Peter, they'd managed to keep Race out of circulation so far, but the strain was really telling. One more day was probably the limit.

Through the small hole bored in the solid wooden door – how much, he wondered irrationally, would the library service claim for that? – he saw four people come through the main doorway of the building and into the foyer. W.P.C. Tuckett, dressed in a smart green frock, offered them one of her pamphlets. The two women shook their heads, one man made a remark at which he laughed, the other man hurried past with the half-defiant, half-apologetic expression of an Englishman who was determined not to suffer proselytization.

He felt sweat trickle down from his armpits. How many years was it now since he had last sweated from tension?

There were three exits from the lecture hall which was up on the first floor. The main one was reached from the head of the stairs leading up from the foyer: the two smaller, emergency ones were on the east and west sides of the hall and there were one-way doors giving access to outside stairs. Three explosive fire bombs, he judged. The uniform sergeant who was to-night lecturing on 'Common faults in the family car' had no idea that his fellow policemen believed the hall was to be bombed. As someone had said, had he known this he might have become a bit distraught and confused the brakes with the accelerator, with dire results.

The bomb expert, waiting in one of the parked cars, had estimated that each bomb would call for a carrying capacity of about one cubic foot. So look for a man with a large brief-case, a small suitcase, or a medium-sized parcel. Everyone in the building, police and civilians, knowingly or unknowingly, was relying on the watchers outside picking out in time the men who were carrying the bombs. . . .

Was P.C. Chase, sitting close to Fusil but no more

than a dark shadow, fingering the Webley he was carrying? Fusil had watched him draw the revolver from the divisional armoury. A quiet, rather dull man, careful of movement, showing no feelings at being called on to arm and perhaps to shoot to kill. Aim at the belly, Fusil remembered once being told on the range: there's more to hit there, especially if he's a beer drinker.

Two men, very deep in conversation, reached the outside doorway. One of them carried a brown paper parcel, but this was no more than six inches long, three deep, and three wide. W.P.C. Tuckett offered them a pamphlet and each took one, still talking and careless of what it was they had just accepted. As they reached the foot of the stairs, they went out of Fusil's sight.

He looked at his watch and the luminous hands showed one minute after the half hour. The uniform sergeant would be standing by the rostrum in the lecture hall, waiting to start. 'Ladies and gentlemen, the basic rule of all vehicle maintenance is, check tyre pressures, oil, water, and battery levels, at least once a week . . .'

'George,' came the murmur from the transceiver, whose volume had been turned down to minimum, which had been put on the small desk. 'Stand by. Six out.' The sergeant and the P.C.s stood.

As Fusil stared through the small hole in the door, he thought: Shock the man so thoroughly that his reactions are frozen long enough to get out and surround him and make him realize that he can't set off the bomb without blowing himself up as well. Hopefully, being a villain, he wouldn't be made of the stuff of martyrs. . . .

'George. Relax. Six out.' The sergeant and the P.C.s sat.

He discovered that the muscles in his arms and legs had been so tensed that now they were shaking.

A P.C. coughed. Another P.C. moved and his chair creaked. 'Go out and tell 'em you're waiting here, instead of just hinting,' whispered the sergeant furiously.

The lecture was scheduled to last an hour and there was a further half-hour for discussion. An hour and a half during which the mob would make their play – if they were going to. They might not believe the *Gazette*: they might have had the house in Astrid Road under surveillance: they might have learned from neighbours that a number of men visited it the evening on which poor Mr Race had had his terrible accident. Right this moment they might be torching a restaurant and laughing at the stupidity of the police.

'George. Stand by. Six out.' The sergeant and the P.C.s stood.

If it's another false alarm I'll have you pounding the beat on late turn for a month, Fusil thought. Goddam it, don't you understand what it's like being cooped up in here? We're looking for three men with packages, brief-cases, or suitcases . . .

'George. Promising, but not developing yet. Six out.'

He gripped the handle of the door, turned it back, then released it. He judged from the message that a car had stopped in a strategic position and although several men were in it, none of them had so far climbed out. Businessmen on their way to an expense-account dinner? Members of a rugger club on a night out, wondering which of the city's four strip clubs offered the hottest menu?

'George. Three with parcels, moving off. Six out.' Even through the tinniness of the transceiver, the tones of excitement were obvious.

He gripped the door handle again, but this time did not turn it. The bomb expert had said: 'The timing

182

mechanism will be a simple one, easily activated on the site to allow the bomber to cope with any unforeseen difficulties on his way to the plant. It may be a clockwork or electrical switch started by pressure from the outside with a short lag, or it may be an acid container and when the parcel is upended the acid works on a very thin rubber cap, eating through this to ignite a chemical mixture which sets off the detonator. I prefer the former, but don't forget to watch for an attempt either briefly to press down on the container or to up-end it.' Forget? None of them would be thinking about anything else.

'George one. Three separating. Six out.'

It surely had to be the bombers. Three of them, peeling off to their target areas, the three exits to the lecture hall.

As the transceiver said, 'George one, now. George two, approaching,' Fusil saw a man come into view as he approached the doorway. Dressed with just a hint of flamboyance: the litheness of someone in good physical trim: apparently at ease, but with the give-away which so often identified both villain and police-man, too interested in everything about him.

The man climbed the steps, parcel in his right hand.

Fusil flung open the door, deliberately letting it crash back to make a sudden noise. 'We're police officers and some of us are armed. Stand quite still and do not try to put that parcel down on the ground.'

The man turned his head and looked at Fusil and his expression was of shock and of hatred.

.   .   .   .   .

It was nearly three in the morning before Fusil arrived home. He left the car in the drive because the garage doors squeaked and entered the house with all the traditional care of a late reveller trying to evade discovery. He was half-way to the stairs when the sitting-room door opened and Josephine hurried out. 'God, Bob, why in the hell didn't you phone me? I've been going out of my mind with worry, imagining the most terrible things.'

He held her tightly to himself. 'You can stop imagining,' he said softly. 'We landed the bombers earlier tonight, but it's taken until now to sweep up afterwards.' No more, he thought, with deep, loving thankfulness: no more will I have to imagine you caught in a fire, writhing in agony. . . .